FOOLISH *love*

KATRINA MARIE

Wee One said I needed to dedicate this book to her. Love you, kid.

prologue

TODAY IS THE DAY. Alex is finally transferring to the same college as me. I never thought this day would actually get here. Or that it would even happen. There have been so many bumps to get this process going.

"Staring at the door isn't going to make him get here any faster." Kate moves into my line of sight with her arms over chest.

"I know that," I scoff. "I'm just ready for him to be here."

"So, you can ditch us and hang out with your high school sweetheart nonstop?"

"That's not fair." She knows how hard this has been for me.

I was devastated when I found out he wasn't accepted here because he missed the deadline date, but that he could transfer in. Though I could have sworn I told him I was applying to Hilltop University. It's not a difficult school to get into. Maybe he didn't hear me.

None of that matters though. He'll be here for the Spring semester, and we can figure things out from there.

"I know," Kate sighs and plops onto the bed next to me. "It was nice having you mostly to ourselves, though."

Rolling my eyes, I rest my head on her shoulder. "You know good and well I'll always make time for you and Samantha. It'll be no different than when we were in high school."

"Except now you have the freedom to do whatever you want without the watchful eyes of your parents. They aren't here to disapprove of your relationship."

Now that I think about it, maybe my parents had something to do with him not applying to Hilltop. They've disliked him since the day we got together. In their eyes he's never been good enough, and never will be. But, I'm certain they would feel that way about anyone I dated. Not that I would know. He's the only guy I've ever had a serious relationship with. Here we are three years later, and an entire future ahead of us.

The door opens and I jump up, ready to greet my boyfriend. It's not him, though. Samantha rushes inside and closes the door behind her. "Is he here yet?"

"I don't know who is more excited...you or Emily." Kate groans.

"Definitely me," I raise my hand like we're in school. I mean, technically we are, but classes don't start for another week.

"Why don't we go eat or something while we wait for him to come in?" Samantha moves to my desk to grab my purse. "Watching the door won't accomplish anything."

"Fine." I know they are trying to keep me occupied, but I've been waiting on this day for six months. Seeing Alex over winter break wasn't enough. We have a lot of time to make up for. "Food first, then we can figure out what to do from there."

Kate hops off the bed and grabs her phone. Her fingers press various buttons on the phone before she tucks it into her pocket. "Let's get out of here. I sent a text to Alex to let us know when he's close."

"What did it say?" I reach for her pocket, but she twirls out of my grasp.

"To hurry up and get here so his love sick girlfriend will stop watching the door."

"I'm not love sick." I grab a pillow off my bed and toss it at her. "I'm excited. There's a difference."

"If you say so." Samantha laughs and rushes to the door. "Let's go."

I've stalled long enough. Alex will get here as soon as he can. The girls are right, waiting by the door isn't going to make it happen any faster.

"I want Mexican food." I yell as I follow my friends out the door.

It's been hours since we left the dorms, and I still haven't heard from Alex.

"Has he called you?" I ask Kate since she was the one who sent him a text earlier.

"Nope." She points to the phone in her hand and at me. "You would have heard it ring, too."

She's wrong though. I would see the faint screen light up, but I wouldn't hear it in this bar. We got tired of taking up a table at the restaurant and decided to head to one of the local bars that allows people under twenty-one. Karaoke night is one of our favorites, and we thought it was a great way to pass the time. Except now... time is crawling by. Not even the energetic performances are enough to pull my attention away from the phone in Kate's hand.

"I'm gonna head back to the dorms." I point toward the door of the bar.

"We'll come, too." They don't argue to stay, and I wonder what they know that I don't.

"You don't have to."

"Please." Samantha snorts. "Like we'd want to enjoy all this amazing signing without you. Where's the fun in that?"

"Fine." I shake my head. "We should probably grab some snacks before we get there, though. I haven't had a chance to stock up the mini fridge."

"Yeah, because you've been too busy staring at the door." Kate grips her phone as she gets out of her chair.

"You live there, too."

"Yeah, but you have an allowance."

She's not wrong. I don't have to worry about anything. Technically Kate doesn't either, but she refuses to use her parents' money. Sam...she didn't have a lot growing up and is cautious with her spending.

It doesn't take us long to get back to the dorms, even with a stop at the grocery store. The sun's been down for a while, and the room is dark when we walk inside.

I half hoped Alex would be waiting for me when we got back. He'd be leaning against the door as the ultimate surprise. But...he's not. The lack of communication is unlike him. Any other day he would be on the phone right now. It's odd I haven't heard from him.

We open up the snacks and watch the eighties romcoms we grew up on to pass the time. The TV is tiny, and I swear one of us will need glasses when we get older from how close we have to get to the screen to see anything.

After two movies it's almost midnight. He should have been here hours ago. Maybe something happened. Surely, he'd let me know...right?

I feel around on top of my nightstand for my phone. I'm not quite as attached to mine as Kate is so it's not on me all the time. Pressing the button to light up the screen, I check for missed calls. There aren't any. I scroll for his name and press call. It rings and rings and rings. He doesn't answer.

"What if something bad happened?" I whisper into the dark room.

"I'm sure something came up and he forgot to call. Let's give it until morning. Maybe he doesn't want to call you so late at night." Samantha's words calm my racing heart a tiny bit. That has to be the explanation. It's still weird, though.

"Okay." I move until I'm between my friends, but I don't put my phone back on the nightstand. Instead, I hold it in my hand so I'll feel it when he calls.

The sun streams through the small gaps in the blinds straight into my face. Sam and Kate are on the tiny twin bed on either side of me. I'm not sure how all three of us fit on here, but I'm happy I have them for support.

My phone is still gripped in my hand, and I sit up as carefully as possible to avoid waking them up. So much for feeling it vibrate in my hand. There's a missed call from Alex, and a voicemail. At least he finally called to let me know what's going on.

Pressing the voicemail button, I wait to hear Alex's voice.

"Hey, Em." From those two words my heart sinks. He sounds upset. "I know this is a chicken shit way to do things. But I don't think we are going to work out. I canceled my transfer. I'm staying here for college." The phone is silent for a second, two seconds, and finally he speaks again. "I hope you know I love you, and I want nothing but the best for you."

"What the fuck?" My voice is a roar. A tone I don't think I've ever heard come from my lips.

Kate and Sam jump out of their slumber, looking around for a threat. "What happened?"

"I-I think Alex just broke up with me."

"What?" Samantha's eyes widen.

I don't have words to form. I open my mouth, but nothing comes out. Instead, I press repeat on the voice-mail and hand her the phone. With every second that passes her face falls cementing my thoughts.

She passes the phone over to Kate, and the process repeats. This time Kate adds her own commentary. "That gutless fucking pig. Who the hell dumps someone over the phone?" She moves over to her bed and searches through the sheets.

"What are you doing?" Sam asks.

"Looking for my keys. I'm going to murder him."

Sam wraps me in her arms as the first tear falls down my cheek. Three years down the drain just like that. No explanation...just over. Soon I feel another pair of arms circle me. Kate has joined my sob fest. Thank God my friends are here with me right now. I'm not sure I could go through this without them.

I'm not sure how long the three of us are huddled on my bed. My face is burning from the crying, and this is not how I expected to start out the second semester of college. Kate leans back and grabs the towel off the back of the desk chair. Patting my face, she clears the tears from my face. Doing her best to wipe away the sadness, though I don't think there's fabric big enough to encapsulate all of the hurt pouring out of me.

"Pack a bag," Kate says as she stands from the bed.

"Why?" My voice is raspy from the hours of disuse.

"We're going to the beach."

"But school," I argue.

Sam bends down until my eyes meet hers. "It doesn't start for another week. We can go to the beach for a while until classes start next week."

"But—"

Kate cuts me off before I have a chance to say anything else. "But nothing. We have time. I'll even dip into the money my parents gave me. This is an emergency. We'll drive down to the coast and let the waves pull away the heartache."

I don't have it in me to argue. "Okay."

They pack my bag for me. I appreciate everything they are trying to do, but a week at the beach isn't enough to wash away three years of memories. But maybe it's enough to fake away the pain by the time we come back.

CHAPTER ONE

THIS WEDDING WILL BE the death of me. Not that I'm unhappy to be lead on this particular event. The bride chose me specifically to keep everything organized arrangement wise because I remind her of her cousin. It's also the most talked about ceremony in the indie music industry right now. Which is funny because they aren't even musicians.

"Hey, Em," Kate calls from the office. "Can you come here really quick?"

"Sure," I answer.

Fear that they'll add something else to my plate swirls in my stomach. I can juggle multiple projects with ease, but all the scrutiny has me second guessing everything. I don't want to let down the couple and our business is riding on this.

My steps are slow and steady as I make my way from the warehouse to the office. I'll be so happy when we can get this exactly how we want it. Thanks to the wedding in question, and the folks who have booked us because of them, we're finally able to do that. It's just a matter of time.

Kate smiles as soon as she seems my face in the door frame. "Tiffany just called. She wants to know if you can meet with them at Stella's house."

"I guess." From most clients this would be odd, but not with Tiffany and Spencer. They almost never come into the shop, and we meet them wherever they decide. "Did something come up with Crooked Halo?"

"I have no idea. She didn't say." Kate shrugs. "But it's probably a good thing because Kai needs the office."

"For what?"

"Something about renovations for the shop."

"He has to do that now when he knows we'll be swamped?" I swear most of the time Kai works on his own time and doesn't care about anything else happening in the shop. Granted he knows what he's doing, but sometimes I think he likes to stress test us.

"It makes sense. We'll be too busy to be in the way of the contractor."

"I guess." I take a seat in the chair opposite her. "Is Sam going to Stella's with me? I'm only the point on making sure things get here in time. She wants Samantha as the creative mastermind."

"I'm sure she will. She's out to lunch with Ben right now."

There is a lack of employees here today. "Where is everyone?"

"Kai is also grabbing food. Paula is up front, and

Caroline is at the school with David. He has some sort of program or ceremony. I can't remember what she said."

"It is getting closer to the end of the school year, and he'll be in junior high next year."

"Don't." Kate puts her hand in the air to stop me from talking. "We don't mention how old these kids are getting. It makes me feel ancient."

"That sounds like a you problem." I laugh. "I like to think I'm only as old as I feel, and I definitely don't feel ancient."

"That's because it's just you in the cute little house. You don't have a boyfriend, or kids. You're are surrounded by everything you love and don't have to worry about giving attention to anyone else."

"You don't have a kid, either." I point out.

Her face reddens and she looks down, a hand pressing against her stomach. "Well…" she trails off.

"Hold up." I lean toward the desk. "Are you telling me I'm going to be an aunt again?"

"Shh. Keep it down. I wasn't even supposed to tell you, yet. I was going to make the announcement Wednesday night."

"At a bar?" I deadpan.

"Hey, nobody said I had to drink at said bar. I can still have water and hang out with my girls."

"It's a good thing I'm the one who found out and not the other two. They can't keep a secret to save their lives."

"You're not wrong there."

This bit of news is exactly what I needed to hear today.

"Have you told anyone else? Your parents?"

"We told Xander's parents. They are over the moon excited." She glances down at her hands. "But we haven't told my parents yet. We've made progress with them, but they still aren't the first people I run to for anything."

"That makes sense. What about Kai?"

"He's the worst at keeping anything a secret. I'll tell Kai soon, and I'm sure he'll spill it to everyone else."

"Tell me what?" Kai's voice booms through the tiny space of the office as he walks in.

"That you suck with planning." I cover quickly.

"I'm not planning anything." He sets his bag of food on the desk and his eyebrows crease together.

"The renovation?" How can he have already forgotten when he needs the office today.

"Oh, yeah, but that's not gonna interfere with anything y'all do."

"You better hope it doesn't." I point my finger at him. "We have a massive event coming up."

"I know, I know."

"Which I should be getting to." I stand and move around the desk to give Kate a quick hug. All the while Kai is looking at us like he's confused. "I'll text Sam on the way out."

"Tell everyone I said hello." Kate waves at me. "I'll help Paula cover the front and handle any orders that come in."

"Thanks. Take it easy, though."

"Would someone tell me what's going on?" Kai glances between the both of us.

"Make sure the contractor you hire is efficient and can hit deadlines." I point at him before turning toward the front of the shop. Keeping this secret will be torture, but I know I can handle it. I only have to stay quiet for a few more days.

Stella is holding the screen door open as soon as I put the car in park. This woman has no chill when people come over. Well, when friends come over. She may not have grown up here, but she's a vital part of our community. Being friends with her is in everyone's best interest.

"It took you long enough," she hollers as I get out of the car. "Do you have any idea how hard it is to keep Tiffany out of the brownies I made?"

"If they're as good as the last batch, I imagine it's pretty difficult." I close the car door and hurry up the porch steps.

"Of course they are." She puts her hand on her hip. "Why would I serve horrible brownies?"

"You really didn't need to bake anything." I laugh. "I'm here on work time, not personal."

"Baked goods are always a good idea. There doesn't need to be a reason."

"You aren't wrong there." I step through the doorway. "Where's Tiffany and Spencer?"

"In the living room." She shakes her head and sighs. "It's the only place I could trust her not to scoop the brownies out with her hands."

I love the camaraderie she has with her cousins. I don't have many, and none that I really speak to. It reminds me of my friends. We're all vastly different, but on the same page when it matters.

Following Stella into the living room, it takes everything in me not to double over in laughter. Tiffany is sitting on the edge of the sofa with a brownie in her hand.

"I was gone less than two minutes. How in the hell did you get that?" Stella is annoyed, but the small tug at her lips lets me know she's not really upset.

"I have my ways." Tiffany shrugs. She glances behind me. "Where's Samantha?"

"She'll be here soon. She was having lunch with Benjamin. I didn't want to interrupt that."

"Oh, I see." She wriggles her eyebrows up and down.

"Not like that." I roll my eyes. Pulling out my notepad I sit on the loveseat across from Tiffany and Spencer. "Do y'all have any questions about the timeline? The wedding will be here before you know it."

"Not really," Spencer says while Tiffany answers, "Yes."

Her husband to be glances at her, "I thought you agreed to all the dates that were sent over?"

"I did, but then I saw a flower arrangement on social media and I might want to use something similar for our wedding party."

"Great, do you have a picture saved so we can see if it's feasible?"

"Um, no. I forgot to do that. But I promise I'll look for it and send it over to you."

"Honestly, I'd let Sam be in charge of that. She'll tell you which flowers will look good with the wedding vibe, and flowers you've already picked out. Especially since it won't exactly be traditional."

"She can do that?"

"Yep." I nod. "She's pretty amazing when it comes to knowing what people need."

"Cool, cool." Tiffany nods her head. "Is there a certain date we need to have that nailed down? I don't want to put more stress on y'all because I found something I want to add. I'd feel horrible."

"You have no reason to." Stella holds a plate with a brownie in front of me. She'll force it on me if I don't take it, and I honestly don't want to fight it. "You're in good hands with us. Besides, at this point we'd bend over backwards to make sure you have everything you want. You have no idea how much business we've gotten simply because y'all are tying the knot."

"That's actually surprising. We aren't even part of the band," Spencer says before stealing a piece of brownie off his fiancée's plate.

"But you're a fan favorite. Y'all don't realize how much the fans love your relationship. It's actually pretty cute." And it is. Stories like theirs are the reason I love that we've opened up to weddings. Even though I haven't been in a relationship in a while doesn't mean I don't love, love.

"Thank you for working with us in pockets of time. I know our schedules aren't the best, especially with us living hours away."

"Not for long, though." Tiffany grins. "We bought a

piece of property down the road and will start building when Crooked Halo is on a break."

"That's awesome." Looks like the town will grow by two more. If things keep booming out here the way they are, we won't be much of a small town anymore. "Are y'all going to take care of the Crooked Halo stuff from here?"

"Honestly, I do most of it online anyway." Spencer shrugs. "But I'll still go to shows when I can. It's been a wild ride handling their marketing and promotion. I just want some down time to enjoy with Tiff."

His eyes linger on her, his fiancée, and I love that you can tell how much he loves her by that one look.

"Makes sense." I'm not sure what else I'm supposed to do. Sam isn't here yet, and I can't really do much except for set dates for delivery. "I'll get the exact dates down for your flowers to be here. It shouldn't be too much longer since the wedding is just a couple of weeks away."

"Who are you bringing as a date?" Tiffany leans forward, eager for my answer.

"Um, I'm a vendor at the event. I don't typically attend after I have everything set up." I did get a wedding invitation from her, but I thought it was a courtesy. Never did I think she would want me to be a guest.

"You are also a family friend, which makes you someone we wanted to invite. You, and the girls are the only ones we haven't heard from yet."

Whew, I let out a sigh. At least I know I'm not the only one who thought it was only a gesture. "I'm not sure. I'm not really dating anyone."

"Well, you better get on that. You don't have long." There's no way I'm bringing some random person as a date to her wedding.

I open my mouth to argue, but Stella shakes her head. "There's no use making a fuss. Tiff is stubborn, and if you try to leave after set up, she's likely to find you and drag you to a seat in her wedding dress."

"Yep." Tiffany grins. "I have no shame. Now, make sure the rest of the Daisy crew gives us an answer soon. We need to make sure there's enough food and booze."

She may be bossy and unconventional, but at least she knows how to party. "Okay, I'll make sure we get them dropped off in the next few days."

"And yours better have a plus one on it." She holds her hand up to let me know there's no room for argument. "I don't care if it's a fling or someone you have a crush on. Live a little."

That last comment is a soft punch to the gut. I do live. I have my friends, family, and a few hobbies. I don't need someone around all the time to complete me. Casual dating is where it's at for me. But maybe Tiffany's insistence will push me out of my comfort zone. Either way, it's a goal I'm willing to accept.

"Do you need anything else?" I ask before standing.

"Nope." Tiffany shakes her head. "Your RSVP and dates the flowers will be here. How will you set them up? Will it be inside and outside?"

"Yeah, I have a few designs. Once Sam gets with me about the small tweaks you want to make, both of us will make sure everything works and email you the idea."

"Sounds good." She waves now that the important bits are done. "Don't forget, find a date."

With those parting words, I head toward the door. I never realized how bossy she can be when she puts her mind to it. She's more intense than Stella, and I didn't think that was possible. I guess finding a date has moved to the top of my to do list in the upcoming weeks.

NEVER IN A MILLION years did I think I'd return to Asheville. Especially not to stay. It's both different and the same as it's been for my entire life. I guess the right word would be updated. It's like the entire town has had a facelift since I've been away.

"What has you over there deep in thought, son?" My dad asks from the recliner. He's watching a baseball game, and I have no idea who is winning.

"Nothing. It's just weird being back here." I swore all those years ago I'd never come back. I guess life has a funny way of working out.

"You've been here for a month, and you haven't ventured out. Maybe you should check out some of the new businesses."

"Most of them are the same as they've always been, Dad. I doubt that much has changed."

"Out of the Ashes had a nice makeover."

Why is this man insistent on me getting out of the

house? It's not like I can do much, I have other priorities now. Kira is my priority, and him and mom are too. He may not think they need my help, but they aren't getting any younger.

"Is there a reason you keep bringing up the bar? I'm not exactly in my partying days anymore."

"Nobody said you had to go and get shit faced, Alex." Dad shakes his head at me.

"And what am I supposed to do with Kira?"

"Well, if it's during lunch you can take her with you." He shrugs. "Otherwise, me and your mom are perfectly capable of watching her."

I'm not so sure about that. She keeps me on my toes on a daily basis. After she hit the toddler stage, she never stood still. But taking care of her on my own past that... has been interesting.

"Daddy," her voice screeches through the small house.

I jump out of my chair and rush down the hallway to the bathroom the two of us are sharing. "What's wrong, honey?"

A quick glance over her shows she's not physically hurt or anything. Though it's hard to know for sure with all the bubbles filling the tub. She points to the corner of the bathtub, and looks up at me. "There's a lobster in the bath."

"Kira, I don't see anything."

This isn't the first time she's gotten overexcited about some imaginary animal in or around the house. Well, in general. There was one time we were driving home from the grocery store and she swears she saw monkeys in the tree, and I have no idea why. Maybe it was the zoo trip we had earlier in the week I don't know. But there's never a dull moment with this child.

"It's right there."

She sighs and lifts her hands to my face. With one hand on each cheek, she turns my face toward the corner of the bathtub.

"Daddy. It's right there."

It takes me a second to recognize the seriousness in her voice, and focus on what she is trying to show me.

A scorpion is hanging out on the side the bathtub. "Oh my God." I mutter as I lift Kira out of the tub and wrap the towel around her as quickly as possible. Bubbles and all.

"Mom, can you come take care of Kira really quick?" I yell hoping my mom can hear me.

Within seconds, I hear her in the doorway. "What's wrong? Is she hurt?"

"No." I shake my head. "You have a scorpion problem."

I turn toward my mom and can see she's shivering at the thought of having these stupid creatures in her house. I remember them being an issue when I was younger but we've never had one in the house. They were always outside in their natural habitat.

"Did it sting her?" Mom asks as she motions Kira toward her.

"No, I don't think so." My eyes are focused like a laser beam on the tiny creature to make sure it doesn't move.

"Can you finish getting her ready for bed while I deal with this?"

"Yeah, no problem." She pauses outside the door and laughs. "It looks like she'll have a fun story to tell her friends."

Of course, my mom is always looking on the bright side. Finding a scorpion in your bathtub is definitely not a fun story.

I remember the first time I encountered one. I was just a kid and it was crawling on my leg while I was sitting outside. I haven't liked them ever since. It's one of the few things I didn't miss about living out here.

Now, how the hell am I going to trap this thing?

I don't want to lose sight of it, because then I may never find it again. And I'll be walking around the house paranoid it'll sting me.

I glance around the bathroom and see a cup holding the toothbrushes on the counter by the sink. I dump the toothbrushes onto the counter and hurry back over to the tub.

The scorpion must be able to sense what I'm doing because it curls its tail forward. But I slam the cup over it before it has a chance to do anything, and push the cup closer to wall so it won't fall off.

I don't know how I'm gonna get it from there to outside but for now this works.

Swiping away the bubbles, I find the drain cover and lift it to let out all the water. I feel confident enough to leave the bathroom to find another cup or bowl to finish my entrapment.

I'm back within a couple of minutes. The cup hasn't moved, which I don't know why I would think it did. That cup is heavy, and I don't think that little scorpion is strong enough to push it. It's not like he's some supervillain.

I lean across the bathtub, doing my best not to get soaking wet in the process and tilt the bowl to the ledge of the bathtub. Slowly, I slide the cup over until there's barely an opening underneath it.

Finally, the scorpion drops from under the cup into the bowl, and I let out a deep breath.

It's crawling around the bowl, trying to figure out what's happening, or get out. I don't know, but it's very creepy. But this is also a learning lesson for Kira.

With the bowl in hand, I walk out of the bathroom and turn toward the hall and Kira's room.

After getting over the fact, I'm holding a scorpion in my hand, even if it's in a bowl, I knock on her bedroom door. "Are you decent?"

I can hear her giggle through the closed door. "I'm always decent, Daddy."

This kid has jokes. "You know what I mean. Are you dressed?"

"Yep, I'm in my jammies."

My mom opens the door before I have a chance to and gasps as soon as she sees the scorpion in the bowl. "That thing is huge."

"I know. But before I throw it out, I want to show Kira what it actually is."

"That's probably a good idea." Mom agrees.

"Did you catch the lobster?" She asks, acting like it's no big deal.

"Yes, I caught it." My grip on the bowl tightens so she doesn't try to jostle it out of my hands. "Come here. I want to show you what it looks like up close. That way you know how to spot them and won't mess with them."

She moves beside me and leans over the slightest bit to get a better look. "Why does it have a pointy thing on its tail? Lobsters don't have those."

"Because it's not a lobster, Kira. This is a scorpion. You've probably never seen one of these. But they do sting." She lets out a tiny gasp and takes a small step back. "And it'll hurt if that happens to you."

"But they have claws like a lobster. Do they pinch, too?"

"Yes, they also pinch. But if you see one come get me, Grandma, or Grandpa and we'll take care of it."

It's hard saying that with a straight face because I know there's no chance in hell my mom is going to handle a scorpion.

Though she might when it comes to her granddaughter. I've noticed Kira gets away with a lot of more things than I did when I was a kid.

"Okay, I'll let you know." She glances around the room for a moment. "Can we keep it?"

Of course, that would be the question that comes next. Because my daughter wants to keep all the things she finds.

"No, we can't keep it."

"Are you going to kill it?" Her voice is low and full of concern.

Despite wanting to kill it, there's no way I can now. "No, I'm not going to kill it. After I get you tucked into bed, I'm going to walk a little way down the road and release it back into the grass."

"That sounds like a good idea." Kira nods.

"Mom, you want to take this while I put her to bed?"

My mom holds her hands up in the air. "No, thank you."

I'm not surprised at her answer. It was worth a shot, though.

"Fine." I set the bowl on Kira's dresser and grab the book we're reading from the shelf.

"Can we read more than one chapter tonight?" Kira asks as she climbs into bed and gets settled.

"I don't think so, Honey. I need to go deal with the scorpion." I wait for her to pull the blankets over herself. "And figure out ways I can keep them from coming inside.:

"Oh, okay." She waits until I'm sitting down next to her and snuggles into my side.

I do my best to raise my voice to sound like the young girl in the book. It's something about babysitters and trying to raise money for some type of program. It's not my cup of tea, but she loves it, and that's all that matters.

These are the memories I have of my childhood with my mom that I want to pass down to Kira. Although, I'm surprised my mom isn't fighting me tooth and nail to get this honor.

Kira's asleep before I finish the entire chapter. I slide the bookmark back into place and set the book on her nightstand. Sliding out of the bed, I pull the covers up the rest of the way. A quick kiss on her forehead, and I pause long enough to grab the scorpion and tiptoe out of her room. She's a light sleeper, and I don't want to go through the whole process again.

"So, are you going to explore the town a little tomorrow?" Dad is still on about this conversation. I thought we'd cleared that up when we talked earlier.

"No, dad. I'm not going to explore the town or to the bar." I don't know why he keeps pressing me about this. It's not something I need to deal with right now. "The first thing I'm going to do in the morning after I dropped Kira off at school is find pesticides that work against scorpions so we can keep them out of the house."

"It's never been a problem before." Dad shrugs. "At least not that I can remember."

It probably wasn't. But he doesn't take care of the place like he used to. That's why I'm here. That and the fact that Kira's mom left and never came back.

I wanted her to have the upbringing I did. Plus, it's so hard trying to raise a child in the city on your own. Not very many babysitters or daycare centers work well with the hours that I have with my construction company. Here, I don't have to worry about that.

"It's fine. In fact, once were completely settled, I will go to the places I promise."

"I think a month is enough time to settle. It's not like you're brand new here."

I'm not but getting settled isn't the only reason I want to avoid anything in town for long periods of time. I also don't want to take the chance of running into Emily.

There isn't a good way to broach the subject of what happened to us when it does happen. And I don't want that to happen in public. Who knows, maybe things will change between now and then.

Right now, I don't have the nerve to see her, or deal with a confrontation that I know is coming my way.

CHAPTER THREE

"TIFFANY BETTER BE glad we love her because the flowers she wants for the bridesmaids and groomsmen isn't the easiest to find." Samantha furiously clicks the mouse on the computer.

"We can always special order them if we need to." I suggest. "It's not like we haven't done it for brides before. And those are ones we didn't really like."

"Please." Sam scoffs. "I don't think there's anybody you don't like. You have never lost your patience with a client before. And that's not something the rest of us can say."

"She's right," Caroline adds. "I mean, I haven't offended as many as she has. But there are customers that I have gotten snippy with."

Samantha rolls her eyes at the comment. She doesn't say anything, though. She knows it's true.

Kate joins the conversation. "I just end up doing whatever I want. They either like it or they don't. But I haven't had anybody complained yet."

The four of us are sitting around the work table in the back of the shop eating lunch. Normally, Kai would join us but he's been on the phone all day with various contractors. And Paula had some mysterious meeting she had to go to, but she wouldn't give us any details on what it's about. There's one thing most of us hate and it's the unknown. I don't think there's ever been a time when we didn't know what the other was up to.

Taking a drink of my sweet tea, I shake my head at Kate's last comment. "You might not think they complained. But my inbox suggests otherwise."

"Then they should say something." Kate shrugs her shoulders and takes a bite of her food. "It's not my fault some of them have impossible requests. I try to get as close as possible to make that happen, but I'm also not going to baby them into making their decisions."

Her eyes meet mine, and I know it's a targeted comment. It's one of my downfalls, I guess. Maybe a bad quality? I don't know, but I have happy clients so I guess it works. Despite how much time it takes me to finally wriggle out answers from them.

The room is filled with silence for a few moments. The only sound coming from the bluetooth speaker in the corner. It's nice when we can have these moments. Usually when we're here, it's constant chaos. Now that we've smoothed out operations with our employees and everybody knows what they're doing, it's not as stressful.

"Y'all are coming to David's game tonight, right?" Caroline asks.

The rest of us nod in agreement.

"Yeah, I thought we already established that," Kate says.

"I just wanted to make sure because David keeps asking if y'all have new shirts this season."

"No," Sam answers. "I didn't realize we were having to make seasonal shirts to support him."

"I didn't either, but apparently he thinks each year he plays, your shirt needs to change."

That has the potential to become expensive quickly. David plays all the sports. It's a wonder Caroline and Carlos can keep up.

"I can run to the house and get my crafting stuff. Maybe I can get some shirts made while we're here," I offer.

"You don't have to do that," Caroline says shaking her head. "Just because y'all are his aunts doesn't mean y'all have to give in to his every whim."

"That's exactly what that means," Kate argues. "Anything he wants. He gets it."

"You're going to regret that when he's a teenager." Caroline laughs. "But I'm interested to see how that works out."

"It'll work out just fine because he knows Aunt Kate has his back."

Caroline shakes her head. "I hope you keep that same energy when he's that age."

"Oh, I totally forgot to ask. Have you RSVP'd for Tiffany's wedding?" I should have brought it up yesterday, but I forgot.

Three sets of eyes fall on me.

"Were we supposed to go? I thought the invitation was a courtesy," Kate says.

"Yeah, that's what I thought too, until I met with her the other day. She said she needs all of our RSVPs along with how many people are coming with us. Something about needing to get a final number to their caterer."

"She knows that's not common, right?" Sam adds. "Never once have we actually been invited to the wedding we've done the decorating for."

"I know that. But she insists that after we set up, we be seated during the ceremony and at the reception."

"I wonder why she didn't mention anything to me about that when I came over after you left." Sam questions.

"I have no idea. She was probably too focused on her flowers."

"Well, clearly we all have partners." Caroline motions toward all the people coupled up. "So, who were you going to take to the wedding?"

"Hey." I raise my hands in defense. "I'm not the only single person. Paula doesn't have an attachment either. Why do we have to take anybody?"

I push away the demand Tiffany made rattling around inside my head.

"Because it's been forever since you've been on a date," Kate says. "What a perfect time to have a date go to a wedding, get drunk, then go home." She winks so I get the meaning of what she's suggesting. I'm not dumb.

Before Xander that was totally Kate's M.O. Now, she's happily in love and doesn't need, or want, to go out all the time.

"You know." Caroline leans her chin on her hand. "I've heard rumblings that a certain someone is back in town."

"Absolutely not."

She's not the only person who has heard rumors he's back in town. I haven't seen him and I know these three haven't. But there's no way in hell I'll be asking Alex as my date to a wedding. Not after his broken promise when we were in college, and then ghosting me when he broke my heart for no reason.

"Maybe he's changed." Kate shrugs her shoulders.

"I don't care if he has or not." I grind my teeth and frustration. "I'm not going to give Alex a chance to hurt me all over again." I learned my lesson the hard way.

"We were kids back then." Samantha thinks she's being helpful. She's not. "But I get it. I guess this means we'll all be on the lookout for a date for you."

"And Paula, if y'all are searching for a date for me, you need to be searching for a date for her as well." There's no way I'm going through this alone. They can play match maker with both of us.

"Date for what?" Paula's voice comes from the door.

"Tiffany's wedding," Kate answers. "We've been instructed to bring dates."

That's not exactly what Tiffany said. She only said I need plus one. But I'll let them run with it if it means not going through their scrutiny on my own.

"Oh, no, thank you."

She doesn't even bother staying in the room with us while we finish eating. Instead, she marches right back to the front of the shop to open it back up for customers.

Well, that backfired. She's done with the conversation before it's even started. Why can't our friends be okay with that from me?

I clean up the trash in front of me. "I guess we better get back to work if we want to be done in time for David's baseball game tonight."

"Yep." Kate grins. "Because now Operation find Emily a date is on."

This will be a nightmare. I'm sure of it.

David is killing it on the field tonight. He just got a home run. The season has just begun, and his team is starting it off with a bang.

After our small celebration, we sit back in our chairs to watch the rest of the game. Samantha and Benjamin are being all cute and cuddly, bringing out a side of her I haven't seen since we were teens. It's adorable, and I'm glad she's found her person. Despite being polar opposites, they work well together.

"Whoa, is that Alex?" Kate stands and uses her hand to block the sun from her face.

I peek around her to see if it is in fact the man in question. Shit. What is he doing here?

I tug my cap lower over my face, doing everything I can to shield it so he won't see me. "Sit down, Kate, before he sees you."

She glances at me over her shoulder. "It may be too late for that."

Please, for the love of all things holy, let him keep

walking. Surely, he can't think I'll actually talk to him if he approaches me. If so, he lives in the land of delusion, and there's nothing that will make him come out of it.

Finally, Kate sits down and I have a clear line of sight. There's no mistaking that he sees me. He pauses for the briefest second at the bleachers by us. He lifts his hand as if he's going to wave, but puts it back down and continues walking wherever he's headed. Smart man. It's the one thing he's made an intelligent choice about.

I'm trying to figure out why he's even here. It's then I notice the little girl on the other side of him, holding his hand. Is that his daughter? When did he become a dad? I have so many questions. But they'll never get answers because I'm not opening that box ever again.

My entire goal, now that I have confirmation he's back in town, is to avoid him at all costs. Maybe I'll be lucky and he's only here to visit his parents. I could ask them next time I run into them at the grocery store, but they pretty much know he isn't a topic I like to talk about. I still adore them. It's not their fault their son decided to act like an asshole. I'm almost certain they know as much as I do about why he broke up with me that year in college.

Oh well, It's water under the bridge. I don't need to know.

"Why didn't you wave, or say hi?" Kate whisper yells at me.

"You seriously need to ask that?" Unbelievable. She still holds grudges against her parents about how they differently they treated her and her brother. But she expects me to forgive Alex because he passes by with a little girl in tow. I don't think so.

"Maybe the two of you need to talk things out, and put old things to rest." Caroline leans closer to me so nobody else can hear. "I'm not saying to give him another chance. Hell, we don't even know if he's single. But maybe it'll be good for you to get some closure."

"I don't need that. I'm completely over him."

"Your sparkling demeanor says otherwise." She pats my hand before leaning back to her seat. "Just think about it."

Okay, I've thought about it. I don't need to talk to him. The sooner my friends get that, the better. His name has been off limits for years. I don't see a reason to change that now.

CHAPTER FOUR

WELL, so much for avoiding Emily. That went up in smoke as soon as I saw Kate put all of her focus on me. It's been a couple of weeks, and I can't get her out of my head. I thought about her here and there, but now the possibility of us is nonstop. I know I have to live with my mistakes.

A small part of me wanted to at least say hi to Emily. I even started to wave, but the intelligent part of my brain told me not to bother. From the momentary glimpse I got of her, I couldn't tell whether or not she was happy to see me. But the blank stare didn't exactly help. I don't see any situation where she'd be excited to see me. It's a shock she didn't tell me off at the baseball fields, but she's not the type of person to have public outbursts. At least, she wasn't. I don't know what sort of person she is now. It's been too many years since I've seen her.

"Daddy." Kira is jumping up and down and pulling on my arm. "Can we go practice now? You said if we finished dinner early enough, you would help me practice my batting."

She's not wrong, but it's rained a lot since the other day and there are mosquitoes everywhere. Maybe it's what I need, though. Something to keep my mind off the girl I let get away because I was too intimidated to stand up for myself.

"Okay, grab your bat and a ball. We will practice for a little bit before you have to get ready for bed. How does that sound?"

"Sounds awesome," she yells.

These are the moments I live for. I'm just grateful Asheville had a team she could play on considering we missed sign ups when we moved here. I never really thought she would be one to play softball, but a team where we used to live, came to her school one day and that was all she talked about for weeks.

I'm heading to the garage to get the T-ball stand, but my dad stops me in the kitchen. "You got a call when you were gone."

"Oh yeah, about what?"

"Contracting work." His voice is gruff. As if I should know what the call is about. I wasn't here to take it.

"Do you have any more information?" Dad usually over explains everything, but it seems like right now he's being elusive on purpose.

"He only said he needed a contractor for some remodeling. I forgot to get his name, but this is the address."

"Did you get a number? How am I supposed to know

when to show up at the address if I don't have a way to get a hold of somebody?"

Why the hell is my dad acting so weird? It's not the norm for him, and I have a feeling he's up to something.

"Yeah I can pull it off the caller ID." he points to the phone. It's a wonder we still have an actual landline. Most people don't have those anymore. And it has to be somebody he knows because I give everyone my cell phone number for business purposes and it's listed on my website.

"Okay," I draw out. "I'm practicing with Kira for a little bit. Can you write it down for me? I'll call them first thing in the morning."

"Sure thing." He waves me off. "She'll be amazing at softball when she gets to high school if she sticks with it."

"That's if she likes it for that long." I'm not the parent that pushes sports on their kids. Or any activity for that matter. If she changes her mind and wants to try something else, I'm fine with that. Her mom kept trying to push her kicking and screaming to do pageants until I told her to stop.

"I'm sure she will. There isn't much else to do here except play sports and hang out with friends." He opens the fridge and pulls out a beer. Something he's not even supposed to be drinking anymore, but there's no point in wasting my breath. "You should remember that."

"I do." I remember everything from that time in my life. It doesn't fill me with joy like you'd think. All I have now are regrets.

"Are you ready, Daddy?" Kira runs into the kitchen. "Grandpa, you come play, too."

"Sorry, kiddo." Dad ruffles the top of her hair. "You'll beat me, and you know I don't like losing."

"I'll go easy on you." She laughs and pulls away from him.

"Maybe next time."

Hopefully he means that. I don't think he realizes he doesn't even have to play. She'll be happy if he's standing out there watching her. I get why he doesn't, though. His body can't handle it as well with all his health problems.

"Let's get out there before the mosquitos get too bad."

"They like you way more than me." She giggles as she grabs my hand and pulls me toward the door.

It's good to know my child is willing to offer me to the mosquito gods just so she can practice softball.

⁂

"I'm heading out to look at that job," I call over my shoulder to my dad.

"Who's taking baby girl to school?"

"Mom said she would before she heads to the grocery store."

I swear sometimes it's like they never talk. I don't understand how neither of them ever knows what the other is doing. Not that they have to keep tabs on each other but it feels like it'd be a common courtesy

"Oh, okay." He lifts his coffee mug and takes a sip. "Good luck with the job thing."

"Thanks?" He's still acting weird about this job. We've never been a family to keep secrets, and I have a feeling he's keeping a big one from me.

Opening the door, I walk out and close it behind me before jogging to my car. I have no idea what the job is for, or what all it entails. I feel completely unprepared for this meeting.

Well, it's not even a meeting. When I called the number last night, they didn't answer. But dad said they said to come by at any time. I figure most businesses open around eight and now is a good time.

Besides, going early means the rest of my day is opened up, and I won't have anything else conflicting with talking to the person. Not that I have a bunch of plans anyway. I don't go anywhere, and have zero jobs lined up.

I plug the address into my phone and back out of the driveway. I know the job is in town center somewhere. I just don't remember all the details very well. It's an area I've avoided since I've been home. Apparently, the baseball field should have been where I avoid since that seems to be where she's at some of the evenings.

Driving through the streets of Asheville I can't help but notice how much is still the same and how much things have changed. Most of the businesses are new and some of the buildings seem to have had a facelift.

There are new subdivisions being built the closer you get to town. Before you know it, Asheville will have multiple stoplights instead of the few on the main roads in town. I never thought I'd see that day.

I guess I always expected it would stay the same, or

die the way a lot of small towns in Texas do. But it looks like Asheville is thriving. And it'll only keep growing from there.

I turn onto the main street, following the little blue line on my phone. It brings me to a corner lot on the far end of the street. After parking, I look up at the sign and groan. This cannot be good, and it can't be a coincidence. No wonder dad was being shady when he was telling me about the job.

I'd be an idiot to not know that this is where Emily works. Not only because it's the only flower shop in town, but because this was her dream along with her friends.

This is the business they wanted to start together, and it looks like they did. From the small mentions my parents make about her, it seems like business is booming.

Part of me wonders if she's the one who actually called but Dad said it was a man. So maybe they have another employee there. Or, maybe he's new and he doesn't know the history between me and Emily.

Right now, the only thing I can do is hope she isn't working because she's liable to kick me out of the shop

Taking a deep breath, I turn off my car and open the door. But I already have a feeling deep in my gut that this is going to be horrible...one way or the other.

I pull open the front door and take a step inside, there are a few customers speaking to a lady I've never seen before. She must definitely be new. But I don't see anybody else that I might know. I don't know why I'm trying to figure out who's new or not. It's not like I have any idea. I left Asheville, and never came back. Emily could have an entirely new set of friends. I doubt it, but it's possible.

I wait until she's done talking to the customers and step up to the counter.

"Hi, somebody called me about a construction job."

The girl behind the counter scrunches her eyebrows in confusion. "Let me see if somebody knows about that. Give me just a second."

She hurries off through the door behind her to find some help. I take a moment to look over the bouquets they have arranged around the shop, and various arrangements inside the glass counters.

That's definitely something Emily and her friends have always been good at. I remember for prom Emily refused to let me buy her a corsage. Her group of friends made everything for all of us. I knew then she was going to do something amazing.

A few moments later, I hear footsteps come down the hall, but they sound heavier than the woman who rushed back there minutes ago. When I look up, a face I haven't seen in ages is staring back at me.

"I didn't know if you were going to show up." Kai reaches his hand out to shake mine.

"It's been a long time, man." I shake his hand before pulling mine back.

"You're telling me. You up and left for college and just never came back."

Little does he know that remark is a punch to the gut. Surely, he has to have some clue that things aren't great between me and Emily.

"Yeah, I heard you did the same." Mom gave me that bit of info on a phone call before I came home. She gets all her gossip during lunch with her friends at Out of the Ashes.

"But it seems like we all come back." He chuckles.

"True, and I think I'm back in town for good. My parents needed some help, and I needed out of the city. Somewhere I could raise my daughter with a tight-knit community." I want her to have everything I did growing up.

"Oh, you have a kid. Congrats man." He takes a step back and looks me up and down. "So, are you interested in the job?"

"You haven't told me what the job is."

"Oh, right. Sorry. I get ahead of myself sometimes." He shakes his head and chuckles. "We're renovating the back area to build another office, an actual break room, and a few other things."

I don't say anything for a second while I think over what both of those jobs would entail. It's likely to set them back a little bit or at least take away from some of the space that they may have back there to work.

"Do you think it's a good idea for me to do this job?"

"Why wouldn't it be?"

"Because of my past with Emily."

He rests his hands on the counter and sighs. "We are all adults. If we can't get past petty hurts from the past, then I don't know what to tell you. But you're the only person I trust to do this job. I've called various other companies and they've either given me the runaround.

Or bid me a quote so high, they knew I wouldn't take their business."

"Damn," that's all I can say.

I've known a few contractors who do that because they're too busy or they just want to see if they can screw somebody over.

"How did you even know I was back in town?" It's a dumb question. I know that as soon as it slips from my mouth.

"News travels fast, friend. And I saw you at the baseball game a couple of weeks ago. I figured if you were there, there was a reason and I might be lucky enough to get a hold of you."

"Yeah, my dad didn't give me too many details when he said you had called. He didn't tell me who or where or any of that."

"That sounds about right." Kai shakes his head. "He's been coming in here a few times to order flowers for your mom that never knows what to order her. It's actually quite funny because the girls give him the same exact flowers every time and he can't remember."

"Yeah, that's typically what happens." It is nice to know he still does things like that to show Mom appreciation after all these years.

A few moments of silence passed between us. "Can I see the space before I decide if I'm going to take the job or not?"

I'm going to take it. I know that already. I don't have a choice but to take it. I'm not broke by any means. It's just soon enough, we'll have to start dipping into savings and I want to avoid that at all costs.

"Yeah, sure. Come on." He waves me behind the counter. "It's just through here. There's a ton of warehouse space. I don't know what this building was before my sister and the girls bought it, but whoever it was really misused the square footage."

I'm trying to remember who may have owned this part of the building when I was a kid, but we never spent much time in town.

"So, what do you do here anyway?"

"Oh, I'm the office manager. Business got too big for the ladies to handle and I was looking for a job."

"They entrusted you with that?"

"Yeah, shocking. I know."

"Yeah, because you were the annoying little brother that always tagged along with us. If it wasn't you, it was Reaf."

"We weren't going to let y'all have all the fun." Kai stops at a wide opening in the warehouse. "This is what we're wanting to transform."

I can work with this. It doesn't look like I'll be in the way of their normal operations, and it's plenty of space for what they want to have done.

"Do you want me to come up with some design specs, or do you already have some in mind?"

"I have a few, but I'd love to see what you come up with."

"Co—"

Before the word is completely out of my mouth, I hear something clatter to the floor behind me. I turn around to see Emily staring at me and then Kai.

HE IS the last person I expected to see when I walked into the warehouse. I need to find out why he's encroaching on my personal space.

"Kai can I talk to you for a second?" Ignoring the mess now at my feet.

"Sure thing." He shoves his hands in his pockets, but doesn't take a step in any direction.

"Over here." I wave him toward the opposite end of the warehouse. The one place I'm hoping Alex can't hear our voices.

"What is he doing here?" There's no point in mincing words. I know he always does what he thinks is best for the shop, but this isn't it. He has to realize that I haven't seen or talked to Alex in over a decade. Actually, it's probably been close to two.

Kai runs a hand through his short hair. "He's going to do the remodels in here."

"Why him?" There have to have been many other contractors to choose from. This is some shady shit I would pull with my friends. I mean, I kind of did it with Sam and Ben. But they worked out. They didn't have an enormous gaping hole left by the person they thought they would spend their life with.

"Nobody else called me back."

"You're telling me out of all the contractors I gave you, not one of them called."

His cheeks redden, and he glances at the floor. "They did, well, most of them, but the prices were too high. There was no way we'd be able to afford what they suggested."

"And your next thought was to call Alex?"

"Not really." He shrugs. He reminds me so much of the boy he used to be when he'd tag along on our adventures. "But when I saw him at the game, I remembered he said he wanted to go into that line of work. It was worth a shot."

Can I blame him? Not really. He's doing what he thinks is best for the business. It's why we hired him. But I don't know how this is going to work. Yes, I'm an adult, I know that. It doesn't stop the hurt from creeping back up.

"Can he do the job?"

"He seems confident, and I trust him."

Alex has been gone for years. I don't understand how he knows he can trust him. Only time will tell if he plans to screw us over like he did me all those years ago.

"Okay." It's time for me to put on my facade and act like my heartbreak meant nothing.

"So, I'm not in the doghouse?"

"No." I shake my head. "Just know that if this ends

badly, I will place all the blame at your feet. I hope you're ready for that."

"You've got nothing to worry about." He heads back to Alex, and I follow behind him.

Alex's eyes are on me, and it reminds of all the times I held his attention throughout high school and after. Until college, at least. I still don't know what happened then.

"Hi, Emily." He lifts his hand in a wave.

"Alex." I nod in his direction. "Most of the work will be done with Kai, he'll show us whatever concepts y'all come up with and we'll make our decisions."

"You look great." His hand flies to his mouth and he blushes. "S-sorry," he sputters through his hand.

"It's fine." I'm doing everything in my power to keep my voice from cracking. To not let him know how much those three little words affected me. Bending down, I pick up the supplies I dropped. Could I do it later? Yes, but I need to busy myself, so I don't focus on the way his eyes linger on me.

"Let me help with that."

His feet move out of the corner of my eye and I hold up a hand, "I've got it."

With all the supplies and flowers cradled in one arm, I stand. I've got to get out of here. Kai is staring at me now with one eyebrow raised. He better not read more into this than he needs to. I know they are excited about Alex being back in town and have my happily ever after playing in their minds. But...it's not going to happen.

"Do you have an appointment today?" Kai pulls out

his phone and scrolls through an app. "I have nothing on the calendar."

"Nope." I shake my head. "Well, not really. Tiffany wants me to meet her for lunch in a non-wedding capacity."

"Want to bring me something back?"

"Not especially." I smirk. He's the kid brother I never had, and I always give him a hard time when I can. "Text me your order, and I'll grab it. We can't let you starve."

"The same as usual is fine with me." He nods toward Alex. "We'll finish up here, and maybe I'll join you."

"As if you're going there for anything else than to see Vivian."

"There's nothing wrong with that."

"I never said there was. So, I don't know why you're asking me to bring you something back." I shake my head. I swear Kai does everything in his power to make things difficult. We'll both end up at the same place.

"Fine," he grumbles. "I'll just meet you up there."

"See you in a bit," I wave, and carry all of my stuff one handed to the side door. Do I need to leave right now? No. But I have to do something because I don't really want to be in the same vicinity as Alex. I'm not exactly sure how I'm going to handle it when he starts working on the renovations. Maybe I'll be gone all the time. At least, that's my hope.

***

"Is everything on track?" Tiffany asks as she takes a sip of her Margarita The drink looks appetizing, and if I didn't have to go back to the shop I would indulge. I definitely need it after my encounter with Alex.

"Yep, your flowers will be here next Wednesday. We can start making the arrangements then." I can't believe the wedding that's gotten us more business than we could ask for is finally here.

"As wild as it sounds, I feel like I've been waiting on this day forever. And now it's coming too quickly." Tiffany's eyes are wide, and I think the fear is setting in. It's completely normal. We've seen it time and time again.

I laugh and take a sip of my water. "You and every other bride we've done flowers for."

The anxiety seems to die down some. At least she knows she's not the only one who freaks out.

"So, have you decided who you're bringing to the wedding?"

This is the biggest problem with doing events for friends. They get entirely too personal

"Nope, I haven't. I don't understand why I can't go alone."

Tiffany shrugs her shoulders. "I mean, I guess you don't have to bring somebody but it would be a lot more fun for you and me both." She tilts her head to the side, thinking for a moment. "Yeah, definitely both. I would get the enjoyment of seeing my friend happy on the dance floor and you would get the enjoyment of what happens when you go home."

Of course, that's where her head goes. She reminds me so much of Kate.

"I'm really not that kind of girl. Not that I have anything against casual flings, but I want it to be real."

"You and Audrey are so much alike. I can't even wrap my head around it."

"I'll take that as a compliment." Audrey is the cousin I know the least. She comes to town occasionally, but not as often as Tiffany and Spencer. I have to say the three of them are complete opposites. It's a wonder they get along so well.

"Lucky for her she ran into her high school sweetheart at Stella's wedding and engagement party... literally."

My stomach drops. "And she took him back?"

"Yeah, I'm actually surprised they haven't tied the know yet."

"Oh."

There's no way in hell I'm telling her about Alex being back in town. I feel like that would only encourage her to try to play matchmaker. And I already know as soon as Eric hears word of my high school sweetheart, moving back for good, he will be putting on his Cupid wings and doing his best to make the magic happen.

He may not be from here originally. But he somehow knows all the gossip. Even from when we were kids. I don't understand how that's possible, and yet here we are.

"I'm sure you'll find someone to bring with you. There's plenty of time."

So much for her letting the date thing drop.

"I'll take yo—" My words die on my lips as Kai walks in with none other than freaking Alex. I swear our office manager has a death wish. He knows the history between us, and he still chose to bring him here of all places. Especially when he knows this is where I am.

Tiffany turns in the direction I'm staring. "Well, hello there."

"Please do not wave them over."

Her hand is mid-air when she stops it to glance back at me. "Don't you and Kai work together? The guy with him is a cutie"

Yeah, said cutie stood me up with zero explanation our freshman year of college. He's had plenty of time to let me know what was going through his head. He chose not to say a word.

"He's completely off limits."

"I'm sensing there's history between the two of you?"

"You could say that."

"I want to hear everything." She puts her hand down and focuses her attention on me. "And I mean every single little detail."

This is not what I wanted at all, but I know there's no getting out of it. She's as bad as Stella when it comes to getting the scoop on things. I can only hope whatever gears are turning in her head come to a halt after I let her know my sordid past with the boy I loved with my entire soul.

alex

THIS IS A BAD IDEA. I shouldn't be here. Well, I mean it's not like I can't be here, but I know Emily is here. Even though she was nice enough before she left for lunch, I know my presence doesn't make her comfortable.

"You good?" Kai calls over his shoulder as I follow him toward the back of the bar. There's a table close to the wall, and he takes a seat.

"Um, yeah." I'm not. Not even a little bit. I can feel Emily's eyes on my back. It was impossible to miss her since we walked right by the table she's sitting at.

I sit down across from my old friend, and Emily is in my line of sight. "Can we switch places?"

Seeing me every time she looks up can't be something she wants, and I don't want to make things hard for her. It's the least I can do after the way I ended things between us all those years ago.

"I'd rather not." He doesn't offer any other explanation.

Okay, I have a new goal for my lunch, don't look up. We'll see if I can manage that without being rude to Kai. Honestly, I should have bowed out of lunch. But he wanted to catch up, and it felt good to be back in the fold somewhat.

"Are you sure Emily is okay with me taking this job?" I need to know. Will it change things? No. I need this job. I had an established customer base before I moved back home. Building that up here will take time. Most of these people probably don't remember me. I wasn't one of the popular kids back then. I was the kid from the poor side of town. The only recognition I got was being Emily's boyfriend. She was the poster child for being a good student and kid when we were in school.

She left for school, came back, and created a successful business. I left and never came back. Folks around here are going to be leery of me.

"Yeah, she's cool with it." A woman comes up to the table and before I have a chance to open my mouth, he orders both of us wings. She gives him a quick peck on the cheek, and I'm pretty sure this is the girlfriend Emily was talking about.

"And you're positive about that?"

"For the millionth time, yes." He shakes his head in exasperation. "She knows you're the only person I trust to get the job done at this point. Especially after the way other contractors have treated us."

I pick that moment to look up and instantly regret it. Emily's gaze is glued to me. Her friend's mouth is wide open as she openly glares at me. She must have told her friend the story of how I broke up with her. It was an asshole move. I know that. But I didn't know what else to do. Not with Emily's dad's voice in my head telling me how worthless I was.

The woman from earlier brings to baskets and sets them in front of me and Kai. Food, the perfect distraction from the direction my thoughts are taking.

"I don't think I've ever seen you in here." The woman holds out her hand, "I'm Vivian, and Kai's girlfriend."

Placing my hand in hers, I give it a quick shake. "Alex. And, I kind of figured that when you kissed him earlier. Emily mentioned his girlfriend worked here."

"Oh, you know Emily and the crew." Vivian smiles, and I can see how much she loves Emily and her friends.

"That's actually a sore subject." Kai shakes his head. At least he didn't air my dirty laundry to her...yet. It's only a matter of time before the town knows all the sordid details. Or, at least her side of the story. Which doesn't paint me in the best light. Nobody will know my side until I tell Emily, and that's not happening any time soon. She's not ready to hear it, and I'm not ready to say it.

"I'm guessing there's bad blood?" She winces as soon as the words leave her mouth.

"Pretty much." I take a bite of my wings and groan. I don't remember these being this good when I was a kid. Not that we were allowed in here too often. Angie would sneak us in when we were teens and it was slow. Perks of having friends slightly older than you, I guess. "So, what do you do here?"

"I'm one of the cooks." She grins. "Patrick hired me on when he noticed he needed help. If he doesn't watch it, that kitchen will be mine."

Kai laughs, and pulls his girlfriend to his side. "They can get a little competitive. I fully expect there to be a cook off at some point."

"I'd love to be a part of that." It's not a lie either. I love food, and when it's good, I can't help but inhale it.

"Okay, I never would have thought of that, but now it's definitely happening." She glances behind her. "Do you think Tiffany would let us do it for her wedding?"

Ah, so the woman with Emily is possibly a client. But they must be on friendly terms if she's telling her about how we broke up.

"Let's not get ahead of ourselves. How about you do it here, some other time? The last thing Tiff wants is to have the two of you competing during her wedding. It's her day."

"It was worth a shot." She shrugs. "It was nice to meet you." She waves and heads back toward where I assume the kitchen is located.

"Looks like you've met your match." I chuckle.

"You have no idea." The grin across his face is all I need to see to know he loves this woman with his whole heart. Much like the way I felt about Emily. Still do if I'm being completely honest with myself. Too bad she'll never give me another shot in hell.

"So, when are you going to ask her to marry you?"

His mouth falls open. "Um, uh, I'm not sure. I mean we've been together a while, but I have no idea when I'd even pop the question. Neither of us are where we want to be just yet."

"Let me give you a bit of advice." Like I'm the first person he should be coming to for that. I destroyed the first girl I loved, and my marriage fell into shambles. I'm definitely the last person he should be listening to. "Don't let her get away. If you want to marry her, go for it. There's no sense in waiting for the right time. You never know what can happen."

He tilts his head to the side. "You sound like you're speaking from experience."

I lift my eyes over his shoulder. Emily is talking with her hands to Tiffany, and all the anger I saw in her eyes moments ago is gone. Nothing but pure joy radiates off her. "Let's just say, I made the biggest mistake I could have. The only good thing that came out of it is Kira."

He nods as if he knows exactly what I'm talking about. I doubt it, but I've been gone a while. Maybe he has history of mistakes in his love life.

"Do you have any pictures of Kira? I saw you with a girl at the baseball fields, but didn't get a good look."

"You might regret asking me that." I pull out my phone and show him all the pictures I've taken recently. Most of the pictures on my phone are of her. A few jobs here and there to add to my website, but one glance at my phone and anyone can tell she's the star in my life.

I don't realize how much time has passed talking with Kai until two people come up to the table. Emily and Tiffany stand between us. Emily is, of course, standing beside Kai. Anything to put distance between us.

"We probably need to head back to the shop soon. I'm sure Paula wants to head out for lunch."

"Damn. I guess I lost track of time." He puts all his trash into the basket. "You're right, though."

Crap this means I'll still run into Emily when we get to the shop. My dumb self didn't drive my car over here. Kai insisted I ride with him. He probably had an inkling I would turn the other way and head home.

"I'm guessing you're Alex?" Tiffany lifts a hand in the air in a small wave. "I'm Tiff. Whoopsie Daisy is taking care of the floral arrangements for my wedding."

"When are you getting married?"

"Less than two weeks." She beams, and Emily shares in the joy.

"Congratulations. I wish you and your husband to be an amazing wedding and happy life together."

"Thanks." Her cheeks blush. "I can't believe I'll be off the market...officially. If you ask my cousins, they'd tell you they never thought they'd see the day."

"They can shut it." Emily grins. "You and Spencer are perfect for each other."

Seeing the joy for her friend sends a pang of hurt into my gut. She should be happy like that for herself. Maybe I caused lasting emotional damage. It's not what I intended or wanted, but there's not much I can do about it now.

Kai shakes his head at the women and stands. "We'll meet you over there."

"We?" Emily asks as she glances between me and Kai.

"Alex rode over with me. He has to go back to the shop to get his car."

"Oh."

Renovating their shop is going to be interesting if she can barely handle me in small doses. What's going to happen when I'm there all day?

"I'll probably leave as soon as we get there. I'll need to pick up my daughter from school."

"It's sweet that you do those things for her." Emily adds. I'm not sure why she thinks I wouldn't. Well, I do, but I probably shouldn't say anything.

"Yeah, my mom offered to do it, but Kira likes when I'm there." Even when we didn't live here, I tried my best to be the one to pick her up from school. It's not easy when you run a construction company with few employees, but that's one of the perks of being your own boss. You can set the hours you want for yourself. "I'll just be happy when school lets out for the summer."

"I can imagine." Emily nods in agreement. "It's all Caroline's son has been talking about." She realizes the rest of the people at our table are silent. "We should probably go."

She gives a small wave before turning toward the front of the bar, and heading for the door.

"Well, that could have been worse." Tiffany shrugs. "Both of you need to work on your small talk."

Kai laughs. "This whole thing will be interesting. Though I think if Emily has anything to do with it, she'll avoid Alex at all costs." He nods his head toward me as he bumps into Tiffany.

"I can't wait to see how that plays out." She doesn't say anything else and heads back to the table she was sitting at.

"You realize I'm standing right here?" I hate when people talk to each other as if I'm invisible.

"Yep." Kai nods. "Let's get out of here."

I follow him back out of the bar. I hope Emily isn't anywhere near the front door when we get there. I don't know if I can handle seeing her act as if she has zero emotions towards me. Even if it is my fault.

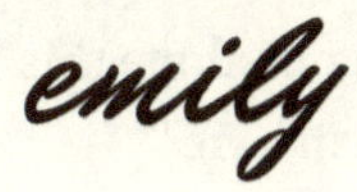

CHAPTER SEVEN

THE SHOP DOOR is unlocked when I put my key in the lock. I'm usually the first one here. I don't see Kai's car anywhere, and the rest of the crew is usually right on time or late. It's been an entire day since I've seen my ex, and I hate admitting how much he's been on my mind.

My stomach drops as I make my way into the ware-house, and see him. Alex is standing by the wall where our coffee maker used to be. He has a measuring tape in his hand, pushing the end up against the wall. I remember him in the same pose when he took shop in high school. Technically, I wasn't supposed to be in the shop since it wasn't one of my classes, but the teacher let us bend the rules. To be fair, he let most of the students have free rein as long as we didn't do anything dangerous while we were in there.

My bag thuds on the work table. Alex stands up, his back straight. I can see the muscles in his shoulders tense. Turning, he sucks in a breath when he sees me.

"Sorry, I didn't realize anyone would be here this early."

We don't open for another hour so I can see why he would come to that conclusion. But I like to get a head start on the orders, and being the only person here is peaceful. Except...I'm not alone this morning.

"How did you get in here?"

He studies his shoes and lifts a hand to scratch the back of his neck. "Kai let me in. He should be back soon. Something about running a quick errand."

Of course he did. I'm pretty sure I know exactly where he went. "He is most likely doing a donut run."

"Ah." Alex nods his head. "Does he do that every morning?"

"Not really." I shrug my shoulders. Nonchalance is the goal here. I can't let him know he has an effect on me after all these years. "He usually only gets them when he's sucking up for something he did."

Understanding dawns on his face. "I guess I'm the reason he's getting them."

"Most likely." Though I won't turn down donuts. I didn't have time to eat anything this morning before I left the house. Getting here and making sure Tiffany's flowers will be here on time is my number one priority. Nothing else matters right now. Not even Alex looking good as hell in those jeans and body-hugging t-shirt.

The warehouse is filled with silence for a few minutes. Doing my best to ignore the weight of it, I pull out the items I need from my bag. My notebook, planner and pens are lined up in a row. This is the only way I'm like Sam. Both of us prefer to make note of things on paper over anything else.

"I see you still like your stationary." His boots thud against the floor as he makes his way toward the table. Of course, that's what he'd remember about our time spent together. Not that we were supposed to be each other's forever. Only the fact I like paper and pretty pens.

"Some things never change." Except everything did at the drop of a hat. I plaster a smile on my face to try to lessen the attitude in my voice. It's hard when I still have so many unanswered questions about what happened that night. Now isn't the time to voice them, though. Mostly, I'm scared to hear the potential answers.

Still, he reads me like a freaking book. He places a hand on the table next to mine. We're almost touching, and despite the sadness and anger I feel toward him, a tiny part of me wants him to slide his fingers between mine.

"I don't have to do this job if it really bothers you." His voice is soft, barely above a whisper. "I don't want to do anything to make you feel uncomfortable."

Too late for that. The words almost tumble out of my mouth, but I have enough sense to hold them back.

"It's fine, honestly." It's not. "Besides, Kai filled me in on the crap some of the other contractors have pulled on him. I know you won't screw us over, and at this point, you're the only person we can trust to get the renovations done."

He winces when I say screw us over. I know he's thinking about the night he didn't show up and broke up with me over voicemail. Talk about being screwed over. I didn't even get a proper break up from him. He took the cowards way out then. Even though it hurts seeing him, taking this job is the least he can do.

"I won't let you down." Again...he doesn't say it, but I know it's meant to be there. There's no way either of us is coming out of this forced reunion unscathed. The only thing I can do is try to keep my feelings at bay, even when they want to creep up on me out of nowhere.

The back door opens, and Alex jerks his hand away from mine. As if we were caught doing something we aren't supposed to. That ship has sailed.

Kai walks in with two boxes stacked in one hand. "I have donuts. Who's hungry?"

Just like that, the tension in the room dissipates. His goofy mood and antics the balm to the hurt bubbling underneath.

"Please tell me you have coffee, too." I glance at the previous location of the coffee maker.

"I have enough for the three of us. It's in the car. Don't tell everyone else." He winks.

"Maybe you should find a new place for the coffee maker until the construction is done. Otherwise, the rest of the group will be coming at you with pitchforks."

Kai shakes and almost drops the donuts. "Yeah, I better get on that. I guess it's going in the office for the time being."

I rush over to him and grab the boxes out of his hand. "Get our coffee first. Then you can set up the machine. And I'll take these so you don't spill them all over the floor."

Kai hurries back outside to get our drinks before

everyone else comes in. Though, if it's like a normal day, we still have a while.

"Is he always like that?" I glance over at Alex as I set down the box, and he's staring after our office manager.

"Most days." I laugh. "Usually, he's trying to figure out if he's made anyone mad so he knows what to do to make up for it. It's usually Sam he annoys. He keeps trying to force her into being an extrovert, and it never works out in his favor. She gets lots of free lunch because of it."

"Do the rest of them know I'll be doing the renovations?" He looks more worried about their reaction that he did mine. Not that I blame him. They are a lot more protective of me than I am of myself.

Kate was ready to search him out and fight him back then. I'm not so sure much has changed. I'm sure she'd still do it if she wasn't so determined to see us get back together. She's changed so much since her and Xander got together. She loves love almost as much as I do. Too bad for me, I may never find it again.

Opening the box of donuts, I grab one of them filled with raspberry jelly. They only make a limited amount, and I'm shocked Kai managed to snag more than one.

"Yep." I lift the donut to my mouth. "I told them after I met Tiffany for lunch." I take a bite and groan. These donuts are the best thing that's happened to me this week. Did Alex react to the noise? I don't know and right now I'm not sure I care. "One thing you'll learn around here is there are no secrets between us. Well, except maybe for Paula."

"Is she the person who works the front area?"

"Yeah. She keeps running off on mysterious errands."

"And none of you have figured out what she's doing, yet?" He reaches for a donut, but pauses before taking one. "May I?"

"Go ahead." I nod toward the box. "Kate thinks she has it figured out, but I don't know if she actually does, or if she's trying to prove that she's smarter than us."

"Y'all are losing your touch." He shakes his head and chuckles. "Y'all knew everything when we were in high school. Usually before the parents or teachers did."

Shrugging my shoulders, I take another bite. "We were a lot nosier back then. Now, we kind of want to do our own thing. Though with some of the flower orders we get, we know a lot of the secrets of folks in town. You'd think they'd use a shop not in their backyard, but half of these people don't have any sense."

"All I'm hearing is this town hasn't changed at all. They like to be messy."

"That's one of the perks of coming home to open the shop. We get to witness everyone else's drama without being a part of it. At least, not directly."

"Interesting take." He laughs before taking another bite of his donut.

Kai strolls back in with a tray holding three coffees. "I wasn't sure how you like yours, Alex. So, it's black, but I brought a shit ton of sugar packets."

"We also have creamer in the fridge." I know he likes his coffee the same way I do. Creamer with a splash of coffee. Or, at least, that's how he used to like it. Things may have changed since we were in high school.

"Thanks." He grabs the cup from Kai and heads

toward the break room. I almost ask how he knows how to get there, but then I remember Kai showed him around yesterday when he was asking about the job.

"You two seem to be getting along much better," Kai says as he hands over my cup.

I take a sip to stall my answer. It's so easy to fall back into easy conversation with Alex. We were together throughout high school, and had he not dumped me our freshman year of college, I'd probably be with him now. As much as the pain still lingers, I still feel a pull toward him.

"There's no point in being a bitch toward him. He's here to do a job. I can be professional while he's here."

Kai snorts before groaning in pain. I glance over at him and he has coffee running down his shirt. "That looked more friendly than being on business terms."

"That's what you get for being a jerk." I point at the dark brown splatter across his shirt. Outside a car door slams. "I'll set up the coffee machine while you try to explain why you have a coffee from the donut shop and they don't."

"You have one, too." He accuses.

"Yeah, but I'll be drinking it in the office and disposing of the cup." I pat his shoulder. "Good luck."

I grab the coffee maker and situate it under one arm before grabbing my coffee and heading toward the office. My steps are rushed as I turn down the hallway, and I bump into Alex. The coffee maker slides from my arm, but never hits the ground.

Alex saved it from a killing blow. "Need some help?"

"That would be great." Anything to get me out of the

argument that's about to happen when my friends walk into the warehouse.

"Can you take my cup?" He holds it out to me. The lid is on it, and he somehow found one of those little stoppers to keep it from spilling.

"Sure." I reach my hand out and his finger graze mine as he hands it over. A shock runs through at me the small touch, and I almost drop the cup on the floor.

Alex gets a better grip on the coffee machine and nods. "After you."

Yeah, there's no way in hell I'm going to survive while he's working here. There's too much history, and it'll be so easy to fall into old patterns.

CHAPTER EIGHT

"DADDY," Kira screams as she gets into the backseat.

"Hey, kiddo. Did you have a good day at school?" I wait until she's buckled into her seat before pulling out of the school driveway. Luckily, everyone at the flower shop was okay with me leaving early to get her from school. Not that they gave me set hours or anything, but it's nice to know it won't be an issue until school is out. Which is only a few short days away.

"Yep." She's bouncing in her seat with excitement. "We mostly watched movies and played on the playground."

"That sounds like a fun day. Can I go back to school?"

"You're too old, silly." She shakes her head at the thought of me going to school with her. I don't know it sounds like a pretty sweet deal to me. No responsibility and having fun. "Did you have fun with grandma and grandpa?"

"Actually, I haven't seen them since this morning. I started work on a job today."

"Ooooh. Is it a fancy house?"

She has to stop watching those home improvement shows with my mom. Next thing you know she'll want me to build one for us. Which isn't a terrible idea. I just need the land for it. Once I get steady jobs again, I'll look into that.

"No, it's not a fancy house. It's actually a store that some of my old friends own."

"You have friends?"

That shouldn't hit me in the gut as much as it does. All she has seen me do is go to work and hang out with her and my parents. Friendships are important and I guess I need to do more to show her that. Though, she's a smart kid and has a ton of friends at school and on her team.

"Yes, I have friends. I just haven't seen them in a while."

She's silent for a moment, and I sneak a peek at her through the review mirror. She's studying the neighborhoods as we pass by.

"You should see them more."

I'll be seeing them a lot since I'm renovating the back area of the flower shop, but I have a feeling she means outside of what I'm contractually obligated to do. The thing she doesn't understand is she's my entire reason for breathing and I won't let anyone distract me from that. Even if that person is the one I know deep down, I should be with right now.

"I'll do my best."

She loses interest in the conversation and starts talking about the movie they watched. It had a dragon that looked like a dog and took place in a story. I don't have the heart to tell her I watched that movie as a kid. Though, it might get us more bonding time. Who knows, maybe she'll think it's cool that we watched the same thing. She's getting older, and a little more opinionated than she used to be.

I have a feeling our dynamic will change some, which is why I shouldn't be worried about being in Emily's good graces.

"Dang it," Mom mutters under her breath.

Dad, Kira, and me are sitting at the dinner table playing a card game. I'm pretty sure he's helping her win. But I can't prove it.

"What's wrong?" I ask as I lay down a card to pick a color.

"We don't have any pasta sauce, and I've already started cooking the rest of dinner."

"Do you want me to run to the store?" It's the least I can do. She helps with Kira so much, and she'll be watching her during the day while I'm working. At least until I can find someone to take care of her.

"That would be great."

I lay my cards face down on the table. "We'll continue this game once I get back." I point my finger at both dad and Kira. "Don't look at my cards."

"Can I come with you, Daddy?" Kira is already sliding out of her chair.

"I won't be gone long."

"Pleeeease." She puts her hands together and bats her eyelashes. How the hell am I supposed to say no to that face?

"Okay, but no wandering around the store. Grandma's already started dinner and needs us back as fast as we can."

"Yes." She throws an arm up in victory.

Rushing to the door, she slides on her flip flops and waits for me to catch up. Within minutes we're in the card and on the road. She asks me to change the radio to one of the local pop stations and she's singing in the backseat to whatever is playing. I don't usually listen to anything other than podcasts and alternative rock, but I can't stop tapping my fingers to the beat against the steering wheel.

It doesn't take us long to get to the grocery store. One of the many perks of being back in a small town. If we still lived in the city, we'd would no doubt be waiting at various stoplights in the amount of time it's taken us to get here.

After parking as close to the door as possible, I turn off the car and turn to Kira. She unbuckles her seatbelt and looks up.

"Don't run off. We're here to get pasta sauce and get out."

"I know, Daddy." She rolls her eyes. "If we don't hurry back, the rest of the food will be ready before we get the main ingredient."

"Okay." I open the door and hurry behind the car to her door. She grabs my hand as she slides out of the backseat and doesn't let go as I close the door.

We only have this small store in town. If we want more variety we have to go to the next town over, but this one has all the staples. I remember working here for a bit when I was high school. Actually, I'm pretty sure most of the people I went to school with worked here at one point during their teenage years. It was almost a rite of passage.

An older woman is walking out the door, and I hurry, pulling Kira along beside me, to hold it open for her. "Thank you," she says as she carries her bags to her car.

"No problem." I nod.

"That was really nice." Kira stares up at me with a wide smile.

"It's always a good idea to be helpful when we can." Like when I caught the coffee maker as it slid out of Emily's arm today. I didn't even think. I reacted. Those girls love their coffee and if that machine would have hit the ground and broken, they would be a force to reckon with.

"Do you remember what Grandma said she needs?" She raises her brows. Sometimes she forgets who is the parent and who is the kid. But I love that she wants to make sure we get what we're supposed to. Besides, it's only one thing. How could I forget?

"Yes." I laugh. "But you can tell me what we need again if it makes you feel better."

She nods and walks into the grocery store. By now she knows this store pretty well. I wonder how many times my mom brings her here. She grabs my hand and pulls me toward the pasta aisle.

Even though the store isn't very big, the shelves hold

so many different sauces. I didn't think to ask her if there's a specific type she gets. I've never paid much attention when she makes spaghetti. It's also been years since I've been home for her to make it.

Kira scans the shelves, taking a step forward to get a better look. She taps her finger against her chin, deep in thought. Walking back and forth she eyes the various kinds.

"Do I need to call her?"

"No, Daddy." She shakes her head. "I'm trying to remember what the label looks like."

"Um, sweetheart, Grandma hasn't made that since we've been living here."

"She has for me."

"When?" I've been home most of the time to avoid running into Emily or anyone else. Not that it mattered since I'm technically working for her now.

"You were in your room being sad." She shrugs her shoulders indifferent.

I wasn't being sad. That and stress are two different things, but I guess I can understand how it looks the same to a kid. I'll have to do better with how I react to our situation, and things in general. The last thing I want is Kira to think any of this is sad.

A hand reaches out beside me and grabs a jar of sauce from the shelf. "I think this is the one you're looking for."

My body freezes at the sound of her voice. What is this? Run in Emily everywhere day?

She's crouched down, handing the jar to Kira.

"That's it." Kira claps her hands before taking the jar. "Thank you."

"You're welcome."

Kira double checks the jar to make sure it is in fact the right one. "How did you know which one to get?"

I cross my arms over my chest, waiting to see how Emily will explain this away.

"I was friends with your dad in school, and spent a lot of time at your grandma and grandpa's. Your grandma makes the very best spaghetti."

"She really does." Kira nods. "It's my favorite. Sometimes she makes it for me after school."

My eyes widen at that. She does not need a full meal as a snack before dinner. Looks like I'll need to have a talk with Mom.

"Kira, this is Emily." I motion toward the woman I've spent so long avoiding. "Emily, this is my daughter, Kira."

"Oh, Daddy has pictures of you in his closet. Sometimes when he looks at them, he gets really sad. You're even prettier than the pictures."

My mouth widens in shock. No filter. I don't know if it's a kid thing in general, or just a special gift my daughter has. As soon as she thinks it, she blurts it out. Embarrassment floods through me. This child is something else.

I glance over at Emily to see if she's as mortified as I am. Though I don't know why she would be. If anything, she must be happy that I've been miserable without her in my life.

But her expression hasn't changed. Her focus is still one hundred percent on my daughter. "Thank you. I'm glad I've aged well."

"What does that mean?" Kira looks from Emily to me.

"It means." Emily's smile widens. "Your dad and I were very young when we took those pictures."

"Why don't you have any pictures as grown-ups? Are you still friends?" The questions tumble out of Kira's mouth.

"Oh wow." Emily stands up quickly. "You're just full of questions." Her eyes meet mine, not knowing how to answer.

"I think we should get the pasta sauce to Grandma. If not, the noodles will be cold." Redirection is the one thing I know how to do really well. Even though I need to have a talk with my child about thinking before speaking.

"Can I get a candy while we're in line?" She's already heading to the end of the aisle.

"Sure." I glance over my shoulder and mouth "sorry" to Emily. She nods, but her face is still blank.

"Bye, Emily." Kira waves to her. "I hope I see you again."

I can almost guarantee Emily hopes for the exact opposite, but she waves. At least she's being amazing about the interaction. Now we need to run away from what is probably the most embarrassing thing that has ever happened to me. I don't know how I'll be able to look her in the face when I see her again.

CHAPTER NINE

KIRA'S WORDS keep rolling around in my head. They were there all night and as I was getting ready for work this morning. He still has pictures of us together. I can't help but wonder what exactly that means. He's the one who broke it off with me, after all. Back then, he was my future. I wanted him to be a part of building Whoopsie Daisy into what it is now. Though, maybe we wouldn't be this far along if we had stayed together.

It's too much to consider and think about. He's a part of my past, and that's one thing the girls have always been sticklers about. We don't stay back there. We keep moving forward onto bigger and better lives. I mean, I think we've done okay in that respect. We're one of the most sought-after flower shops in North Texas. We have brides on a waiting list to work with us. That has to mean something...right?

"Earth to Emily." A hand waves in front of my face. "Hello."

"Would you stop?" I push Kate's hand away. "You could have easily tapped on my shoulder."

"I did." She rolls her eyes. "You didn't respond."

Oh. Crap. He's been in my presence three times and already he's occupying all of my thoughts. How the hell am I supposed to handle him being here daily?

"Sorry. I guess I have a lot on my mind."

"You mean about a certain someone who'll be walking in at any moment?"

I hate she knows me so well.

"No." I argue. "Tiffany's wedding is days away, and I'm making a mental checklist of everything that still needs to be done."

"Sure, you are." She grins. "Besides, we have a solid week before the flowers get in and we really have to pick up the pace. Oh, don't forget girl's night."

She's way too nosey for her own good. I won't give in to her mischievous smile, though. She should know by now it'll get her nowhere. When have I ever forgotten girl's night? It's the one night a week we aren't allowed to talk shop. It's also the night before I have dinner with my parents. I can't believe that's something I still do in my thirties. But outside of the shop, and my friends, I don't really have much else going on.

"Has Sam finalized the designs for the bouquets and table decor?" She'll need help, but she works best alone most of the time. If it wasn't for Tiffany inviting us to the wedding, I'm sure she'd leave after setting up.

Kate shrugs and heads toward the hallway, mostly likely to visit the coffee machine. "I don't know. She hasn't said anything to me. Don't worry. You know she'll get everything squared away before the flowers arrive."

She's right. I don't know why I'm letting this wedding get me so worked up. Maybe because the bride is a friend? Or it could be because it's a high-profile wedding. Oh, I know…it's because all of my friends have a plus one for the wedding and I don't have anyone. I mean, Paula doesn't either, but she's also said she's not taking anyone with her.

Why did Tiffany have to invite us to the actual wedding? There's not a single person who would pique my interest in taking with me.

"Good morning, I brought donuts."

My heartbeat goes into overdrive at the sound of his voice. Okay, so there would be one person. Well, if the circumstances were different. He's from the past. Don't look back. Keep going forward. I have to repeat the words in my head as I turn in his direction.

Alex is wearing a pair of tight-fitting jeans, a black t-shirt, and his work boots. His hair is hidden beneath a baseball cap with pink letters across it. Aside from the hat, it's pretty much what he wore when we were in high school. Always choosing to go the classic route.

"You know you don't have to feed us, right? We're paying you for a service, not the other way around. Love the hat by the way."

He sets the box of donuts down on the worktable in the center of the room, and pulls his cap off his head. "She did it again."

"Who did what?"

"Kira." He shakes his head. "She likes to play pranks

on me, and she switched out my normal cap for the one I wear during her games."

I can't help the laugh from bubbling up. If I'm being honest, she reminds me a lot of our group when we were growing up. Most of us said whatever was on our mind, and always made each other laugh with our antics. But this is something I don't think any of us would have ever done. I'm doubled over trying to get myself under control.

"It's not that funny." He grimaces. "I guess I need to keep my hat in my car from now on."

Another giggle escapes my lips. "Your kid is pretty amazing."

"She is." The proud dad smile that overtakes his face makes him even more handsome. Seeing him now and remembering him then is an odd thing. He's grown into a man I don't even recognize., But he still has the boyish charm that pulled me in when we were teens.

Sliding from the stool I've been sitting in for far too long, I move to get a donut from the box. "How's she adjusting to living here?"

"Easier than I am," he mumbles. "She already has a group of friends, and they are planning sleepovers for the summer."

"That sounds terrifying." I let the bit about him not adjusting well slide. It's not my place to ask, even though I want to. He grew up here. It's odd that he feels like he doesn't fit in.

He shrugs and grabs a donut. Chocolate, his favorite. "If it makes her happy, that's all that matters to me." After taking a bite, he studies me for a minute. "Sorry about last night. She doesn't have much of a filter, and says whatever pops into her brain."

"It's fine." I wave him off. "She took me by surprise for a second, but it's okay."

"Good." He nods. His eyes bounce around the warehouse, trying to focus on anything but me. I'd be lying if I said I didn't wonder what he's thinking. "Is Kai in?"

"Not yet." I shake my head. "He has to take Viv to work. Her car is in the shop or something."

I rarely pay attention to what time he gets in. He's usually an early bird like me, but sometimes he comes in later than normal. As annoying as he can be, it's been good having him here to run the office. This shop really has turned into a family business between all of us.

"Oh, I can come back later, then."

"Is there anything I can do to help?"

"Yeah, is there *anything* she can help with?" Kate comes out from the hallway, wiggling her eyebrows up and down. I swear she's a grown child. "Sweet, donuts."

I grab a roll of floral tape from the table and throw it at her. She ducks at the last second and it misses her. Once Alex leaves, I'm going to murder her. Just because we coerced Sam's love life, doesn't mean she can do the same thing to me. Besides, it's not like I want a relationship. Especially not with Alex.

She sticks her tongue out at me in response. "Thanks for the donuts, Alex. I was starving."

Alex runs his fingers through his hair. His cheeks are bright pink, to match his embarrassment. Though I can't tell if he's embarrassed for me, or because my friend is a jerk.

"I, uh, think I'll wait for Kai."

"Oh, okay. You can hang out in the office if you want. He should be here soon."

"Thanks." With his donut in one hand, he grabs his hat from the table with the other, and high tails it to the office.

I turn on Kate. "What the hell is wrong with you?"

"Nothing." She laughs. "You can feel the chemistry between both of you from the front of the shop." Shrugging her shoulders, she picks up another donut. "I was only trying to help the two of you along."

"Why can't you get it through your head that nothing is going to happen between us."

"You don't know that."

"I do." I throw my hands in the air. Talking to her is like talking to a brick wall sometimes. "Number one, he has a kid. Two, he's doing a job for us. That has to be some sort of conflict of interest. And three, he hasn't expressed any sort of interest in me the few times we've been around each other. Besides, I don't know that I would be able to give him another chance anyway."

"Why? Because he broke up with you when we were eighteen? We were practically kids back then. Maybe we all had a little growing up to do."

"That's rich coming from you."

"What's that supposed to mean?"

Shaking my head, I head toward the door leading to the parking lot. "You are the one who said we shouldn't look backward, only forward to our goals. And he never gave me a reason why he broke up with me."

"One of these days you're gonna have to let that go."

"I'll see you tonight." My hand is on the handle to walk out.

"Where are you going?"

"I'm working from home today." Is it a childish thing to do? Definitely. But I can't deal with her right now.

"Em, I'm sorry." Her words are barely above a whisper as the door slides shut behind me.

The dinner table is uncomfortably quiet tonight. Dad is usually talking about whatever he has going on at the office. Even Mom isn't filling me in with all the gossip in the family. Maybe they can feel the funk I'm in. I'm just glad I was able to clear the air with Kate. Both of us realized we were in the wrong, and it kept girl's night from being awkward.

"How is the big wedding coming along?" Mom asks before taking a bite of her food. Her and Dad double teamed dinner with steak and grilled vegetables. It's probably the best thing about today.

"Really well." Just a week away and everything is lining up perfectly. "Samantha finished up the design for the florals, and now we wait until the flowers come in."

"Are you taking a date to the wedding?"

"H-how did you know we are supposed to take dates? Or that we were invited?" My brain goes into overdrive trying to remember if I mentioned it in passing.

"I heard some ladies talking about it while I was picking up a lunch order at Out of the Ashes."

"Oh." I'm shocked they still go there for food. It's

never really been a place they eat normally, but the food is good.

"Are you taking anyone?" When I shove food in my mouth to keep from answering, she continues, "I have a friend who has a son about your age. Last I heard he's sing—"

"No." I almost choke on my food. "I'm not doing a blind date thing for a wedding. I haven't figured out who I'm taking, or if I'm taking anyone at all."

"As long as it's not that troublemaker you were with in high school," Dad mutters under his breath.

I know for a fact I haven't told them Alex is back in town. Them getting information before I have a chance to say anything is kind of creepy.

"Why would you say that?" My dad has never been a fan of any guys I've seen in my entire life, but he seems to have hated Alex. I wish I knew why, but after Alex broke up with me, I didn't really bother trying to find out. He broke my heart, and when my dad was talking crap, I didn't stop him. Anger fueled everything back then, and I didn't care who was being talked about.

"Because I know he's moved back. The last thing you need right now is to pick up where you left off. Your business is doing great, and distractions are liable to make it crumble. You can't let that happen with a wedding of this magnitude."

My mom whispers something to him in Spanish, and he frowns. Now more than ever, I wish they had taught me Spanish. Dad understands it because Mom taught him. But for some reason they've only spoken English in front of me. Part of me wonders if it's because they didn't want me to know when they were making decisions about me while I was standing right in front of me.

Shaking those thoughts from my head, I turn my focus to Dad. You won't have to worry about that. I'm not looking to date anyone. Much less him.

"Thanks for the concern, Dad, but it's not needed. Another girl from the shop is going alone. Maybe we can be each other's date."

"I just wish you'd settle down like your friends." Mom sighs. "By the time you have kids, I won't be young enough to play with them."

Here we go again. I've never given any sort of indication I want kids, but she keeps forcing the idea on me. Lucky for me, I don't have to sit here and listen to it.

"Wow, look at the time." I tap my wrist knowing damn well I don't have a watch. "I have an early meeting in the morning, and should get going."

"You can't keep running from these conversations, mi vida." Dad sounds tired. They want what they think is best for me, I know that. Except our ideas don't really match up. Forcing me into seeing people and getting serious, isn't the way to go, either.

I rush around the table and kiss Dad on top of the head. "I love you."

Next is Mom, and I know she's upset I'm leaving, but she did it. "Love you, Mom."

Sighing she sets down the fork. "I love you, too. Don't forget to grab the bowl from the fridge, it should last a couple of nights.

"Thank you, and I'll see you next week."

Maybe. They know I can't come over when we have a

deadline on arrangements, and I'm hoping putting together the flowers for Tiffany will take a while. I'm not sure I can handle going through this again. The girls may hate me, but I think I'll be asking them to come to dinner next time. I need a buffer. Though they may bring up Alex, and that will apparently send my dad on another spiral.

All I know is I need to get out of this house. It feels as restrictive in my thirties as it did when I was a teen.

CHAPTER TEN

TWO DAYS. Two days since the awkward moment at the flower shop. I knew exactly what Kate was trying to do. It's what she did whenever she thought her friends had a crush back in high school. It's nice to see some things never change. Even though it looked like Emily was mortified. I don't think I've ever seen her face turn that particular shade of red.

My bedroom door bursts open and Kira dashes across the room, leaping onto the bed. Her elbow connects with my stomach and I grunt. It's way too early for her to have this much energy. If only I could be a kid again for various reasons, not only more energy.

"Whatcha doing?" Her voice is sweet and nothing like the way she entered my room.

"Nothing, why?" Nothing good ever comes from asking that question, but if I don't, she'll continue staring at me with those puppy dog eyes.

"Grandma is thinking about taking me to the movies this afternoon, and I want you to go with us."

"What time?"

"I don't know. She said this afternoon." She sits up. "I can ask her and come back."

"It's fine. I'm getting up now." There are few things I need to take care of this morning.

"Yay." She bounces on the bed in excitement. We really need to talk about boundaries soon. "Grandpa is coming too, so you have to go."

I planned on it anyway, though I'm shocked my dad is going. I guess it's true what they say, becoming a grandparent changes things.

"Why don't you head out to the living room. I'll get dressed and be there in a minute."

"Okay." She kisses my cheek and barrels through the open door.

I throw the blanket off of me and close the door since she forgot. Hopefully the movie is well into the afternoon.

It takes me a few minutes to dress and I join my little family in the living room. "I hear we're going to the movies today."

"Yep." Mom beams. "It starts at four."

"Perfect." I'll have plenty of time to do what I need before going. "Can you watch Kira for a bit?"

"Sure. Is everything okay?"

"Yep. I need to take some measurements for the job at the flower shop, and it's easier to do when they aren't open."

"Just make sure you're back before three."

"But the movie doesn't start until four."

"Yes, but we have to get there and get popcorn. It's easier to get there earlier." Dad chimes in.

"Okay. I'll be back in time." I bend down and give Kira a hug. "Be good for Grandma and Grandpa. I'll be back soon."

"Love you, Daddy."

"Love you, too, kiddo."

Now to finish getting ready so I can go handle my business in peace and quiet.

This is the quietest I've ever heard the flower shop. Even though I've only been here a few times, it's always filled with Emily and her friends laughing about something. It almost feels wrong to be here when nobody else occupies the space. But I need to get measurements now that everyone has signed off on the design I came up with.

It means a lot that they're entrusting this job to me considering the bad blood between me and Emily. Though there are moments I can see slices of the person I used to know peek through. Maybe she doesn't hate me as much as I thought she did.

My measuring tape won't stop bending when I'm trying to get it to the other side of the room. This truly is a two person job. Hell, more than that to get all the work done. I'll have to see if anyone is looking for part time work to get this job done. Who knows, maybe word will get out after I'm finished with this and they can stay full-time.

I walk to the corner of the room and place the end of

the tape measure against it, searching for something to hold it down while I pull the rest of it back to get the numbers I need.

"I can hold that for you."

The tape measure slides back into its case, the metal edge slicing the side of my finger, at the sound of Emily's voice.

I wince at the pain and glance down at the blood seeping through the cut. Nope. I can't do this. Is it a big cut? Not really, at least, I don't think it is. I'm too nervous to focus on it. But me and blood…we don't mix well.

"Do you, uh, have a band-aid?" Keeping my voice steady is difficult and I'm pretty sure I can feel my heartbeat in my finger.

"I guess you still don't like blood." There's a hint of teasing in her voice, and it's so nice to hear it that I forget about my finger for a second.

"Not really."

"We should have some in the office. The amount of times we've hurt ourselves is a little ridiculous." She glances behind her to make sure I'm following her.

I do for a few steps before sitting on the stool closest to me. "Actually, I think I'll wait right here."

But the space is empty. She still knows me well enough to know I won't make it to her office.

She comes back a few minutes later with a small pink box in her hand. "You realize you're probably in the wrong line of work if you can't handle small cuts."

"I don't usually lose control of my measuring tape." And people don't typically sneak up on me. I don't say that part out loud. Her feeling bad is not the way I want this interaction to go now that it's just the two of us.

"Maybe you should hire more people." She opens the box and takes out a small bottle of peroxide and grabs a napkin off the table behind me. She places the napkin under my hand and pours the peroxide over my middle finger. I wince as the cold liquid hits my skin. "Sorry," she says barely above a whisper.

"You'd think by now I'd be okay with wounds. I'm a whole adult now."

"You'd think a lot of things would be possible as an adult, but sometimes it's harder than you imagine."

The sadness in her voice sends a pang to my stomach. Deep down, I know I'm the reason she's feeling whatever it is, but she won't come out and say it. Instead, she dabs away the liquid from my finger to get a better look at the cut.

"I'm so—"

"This cut looks pretty deep. Do you think we should take you to an urgent care place to get checked out?"

I'm almost too scared to look. The pulsing seems to have gone down, but I don't know if that's because my thoughts are on how much I hurt her, or because I'm trying to act tougher than I am.

"As long as it's not bleeding as much anymore, we can put a band-aid on it. If it's still messed up in the morning, I'll go to the doctor and get it checked out before ordering the supplies I need."

"Are you sure?" Worry. That's what I hear. Some part of her does still give a damn about me, even though I know she's fighting it.

I shake my head of the thoughts I'm having. There's no way we can pick back up where we left off all those years ago. Besides, I don't know how Kira would take me dating again, either.

"No, you're not sure? Or, no you don't want to go to the doctor?"

"Both?" I chuckle to her know I'm joking. "I'm sure about not going to the doctor. We're taking Kira to the movies this afternoon, and I can't miss it."

"That's sweet." A small smile passes across her face. She grabs an ointment and rubs it on the wound before picking up a band-aid. "She really is a special girl."

"And also, a menace. Between the pranks and her jumping on top of me first thing in the morning, she may give me gray hair before I'm ready."

"And to think, she's not even a teenager yet."

"Please, do not rush that." I can only imagine what she'll be like as a teen. With us back in Asheville, though, I know I won't have to worry. It's hard to get away with anything in this town. We tried ourselves, and somehow one of our parents always found out.

"Oh, I'm not." She pulls her hand away from mine and cleans up the mess. I'm certain she was distracting me from looking at my finger. "You're all set."

I glance down at my hand at the pink princess band-aid adorning my finger. "Well, at least Kira will like it. Did you do that on purpose?"

"No." She laughs. "Kai kept making fun of us for having a bright pink first aid kit. We took out the boring band-aids and puts these in. Every time he hurts himself or gets a paper cut, he gets to sport these on his finger."

"I'm sure he takes in stride." I shake my head. "He was never one to be embarrassed by anything from what I can remember."

"That man can't take anything seriously. The only reason he works here is because he's family, and he's good at what he does."

"I think it's awesome you have a small, family run business. I don't know much about the woman who runs the front of the shop, though."

The way we can slip back into conversations like we used to is amazing to me. Well, when there aren't friends around to make things awkward. Even though I know I hurt her so deeply when I ended things, but I don't want to tell her the reason for it. It has the likelihood to make her even more upset.

"We hired her over a year ago. Her family owns a winery, and I'm honestly confused why she's not working there, but she keeps kind of quiet about it."

"I guess every family has their drama."

"You're telling me."

What could that be about? Emily's always had a decent relationship with her parents. Probably better than I've seen in most families, including my own. It's not my place to dig into that. At least, not anymore. One day maybe I'll earn her trust back without having to break her heart all over again.

"I better get back to my measurements." I need something to do to keep my hands busy and my mind from running in a million directions when it comes to the woman standing in front of me.

"Let me help you." She pushes the box away and

grabs the trash before sliding it into the can sitting beneath the table. "Clearly, you can't be trusted with a tape measure on your own."

"You don't have to do that." It can't be what she expected to do when she showed up. "What are you doing here, anyway? I thought the shop was closed on Sunday."

"It is." She sighs. "But I wanted to make sure everything is on schedule for the flower delivery this week, and to make sure we have all the supplies we need."

"That makes sense." I glance around the warehouse area. "Do you need any help? I can always wait until tomorrow to take the measurements so Kai can help."

"What are you saying I can't do it because I'm a girl."

"Pfft, not at all." It's wild she would even think that. "I've seen you handle situations I would never be able to." I hold up my hand as evidence. "I didn't want to take away from what you have to do."

"It's fine." She shrugs and lifts up the tape measure I dropped on the floor. "Besides, you have a little girl to take to the movies. We can't have you disappointing her."

Well, that's a jab at our past. But I let it slide because I deserve it. The next few hours will be interesting to say the least.

"I HEAR you and Alex were nice and cozy yesterday." Kate takes a seat between me and Samantha.

"Wait." Carolina rushes from the other side of the room to hear what's being said. "Why were you here on a Sunday?"

Rolling my eyes, I continue putting together a rush bouquet order. It's supposed to be delivered this afternoon, and they placed it twenty minutes ago. I swear we get more last-minute orders than anything else. I need to see if this is an I'm sorry gift, or forgotten birthday.

"I come in more often than y'all think."

Honestly, it shouldn't be a surprise to them. How else do they think things get restocked around here. Kai does his best, but there are times he forgets the most basic things we need to run this place. Like...toilet paper. How does anyone ever forget they need that?

"You're avoiding the question." Samantha pulls the bouquet out of my hand, studying it.

"Because it's none of your business."

"So, something did go down." Kate squeals and claps her hands.

I definitely liked it better when she was single and didn't get all gooey with emotions. Who am I kidding? I'm glad she found someone who matches her on every level. A quick glance around the room makes me grin. I've had a hand in everyone in here finding their perfect person. Aside from Paula, but she's not in the room right this second. I'll figure her out one day.

"You've gotta give us something, Em," Caroline adds before taking a sip of her drink.

This could go on forever if I don't push their thoughts of a happily ever after away.

"Nothing happened. He was here taking measurements, and I came in to double check the orders for Tiffany's wedding. Which we have to start working on tomorrow after they are delivered."

"You didn't know he'd be here?" Samantha scrunches her eyebrows.

"No." Did they forget we made a copy of the key for Alex? It's an agreement we all came to so we wouldn't be called while at a wedding or anything. "He was here taking measurements."

All of them give me looks as if they doubt what I'm saying. I'm perfectly capable of being in the same room as my ex and not wanting to get back with him. Barely, but I managed it.

"Hold on." I grab the bouquet back from Sam. "How did y'all know we were here at the same time?"

Kate focuses anywhere but on me. "Kai may have mentioned he saw y'all on the camera by the back door.

He got an alert when Alex got here, and then another one when you did."

"And that turned into us getting cozy?"

"Well," Kate continues, "Paula may have mentioned she saw the two of you walking out kind of close to each other."

That must be why she hasn't come back here to raid the pastry box like the rest of us.

"Y'all are worse than the little old ladies in town."

"No, we're not." Sam crosses her arms. "We at least keep it within our friend group. We don't blab it out to everyone in our vicinity."

"Only because we're the only ones here."

I drop the bouquet as I throw my hands in the air.

Caroline reaches behind her and pulls the order of the printer, glancing over it and the bouquet. "What I don't understand is why he didn't come take his measurements today. He could have had help."

"I'm one hundred percent sure it's so he could avoid the insanity circling this table. Especially after Kate's antics the other day."

She mutters, "I already apologized for that."

Reaching over, I give her leg a quick pat. She should know that's water under the bridge with me, but he may still be uncomfortable about it.

"We have to make sure we give him the space he needs to work without playing matchmaker. I'm sure he's got a lot going on with coming back to town and raising his daughter, the last thing he or I need is a relationship."

"I'm pretty sure those exact same words came out of

my mouth when y'all kept pushing me to talk to Carlos." Caroline's eyes bounce to each one of us.

"Yeah, but look at you now." Kate grins. "I'm expecting y'all to announce you're having a kid any day now."

"I feel like I've missed that window, and we're both perfectly happy with David. He keeps us busy."

Kate can want another niece or nephew all she wants but I'm happy Caroline and Carlos are happy. In the end that's all the matters.

"That's no lie." I laugh. "I don't see how y'all do it with the schedules you work."

She shrugs and smiles, truly happy in her life. "We have an amazing support system. His family adores mine, and vice versa. If it wasn't for them, I don't know that we could make it work."

"You could always go back to being a stay-at-home mom." Samantha points out.

"I could, but I don't want to. I love working up here with y'all. And as much as I love spending time with David, I need my time away."

"Aw, you love us." I bat my eyes at her before busting out into giggles. "But honestly, have more kids or don't. It's completely up to y'all."

"Exactly," Kate says. "Just like both you and Alex getting over your past is up to you. Is it really that bad of an idea to at least try?"

"We're speaking, and on friendly terms. I think that's good enough." What I don't say is for now. Though, I can tell by their expressions they are thinking it.

"So, what's on your agenda for tonight?" Kate asks. "Xander and I want to head to Out of the Ashes."

"Can't." Caroline shakes her head. "David has baseball practice."

"I'm out. Tonight is dinner with my parents."

"Weren't you over there a couple of days ago?" Kate tilts her head to the side.

"Yeah, but since we'll be working on wedding prep the rest of the week, they are demanding to move it up. You know how they are." All I can do is shrug.

They are amazing parents, but you'd think I'd be able to tell them I don't want to do weekly dinners. It's not like we never see each other. We live in the same freaking town.

"Good luck." Kate laughs.

"Me and Ben can probably go." Sam adds in.

"Awesome." Kate throws her hand in the air. "I'll ask Paula if she wants to go. I'd ask my brother, but we all know he'll show up anyway."

"Show up where?" Kai walks into the warehouse. "Are we getting into trouble tonight?"

"We are if you're going." Kate crosses her arms, clearly not happy he barged into the room.

"I'm in." He doesn't even ask what the plans are. That's one perk of having him around. He goes with the flow without knowing anything.

"I hope y'all have fun. At least we have girl's night."

"For sure. The next few days are going to be...a lot." Sam groans. There's so much work to do, but I have all the faith in the world that we'll get it done.

Knocking on the door, I wait until one of my parents comes to answer it. But they don't. Weird. They are usually waiting on pins and needles for me to come over. I dig the key out of my bag, put it into the lock and turn.

As soon as I open the door, the smell of my childhood greets me. The spices fill the air, and I take a moment to breathe it in before heading straight toward the kitchen. There's nothing like the scent of spices and food. I can get a similar experience at restaurants, but having it at home is even better. Well, my childhood home. I did whatever I could not to have to move back in when I got out of college. I love my parents, but they...are a lot.

Mom is standing at the stove with a spoon in her hand, stirring something. "Hey, Mom."

I peek over her shoulder to see what we're having and almost cheer. Picadillo is my favorite. It doesn't matter than its hot outside. It's one of my favorite comfort dishes. I think the last time I had it was when I had to deal with a horrible bride at the shop. Mom fixed it for me to make me happy.

"Hey sweetie." She reaches out and pulls me into a side hug. "I didn't hear you knock."

"It's okay, I have a key." I hold up the item in question. "Where's Dad?"

"Taking a quick shower. He went for a run before you got here."

It always amazes me how he makes time to go for runs, manage a business and spend time with Mom. I'm doing good to go to work and keep work tasks there.

They always seem to follow me home. His ability to compartmentalize is out of this world. I aspire to be like him, but I know that will never happen. It doesn't fit my personality.

"Do you need help with anything?" I ask as she continues stirring. "I can warm up the tortillas or anything else you need."

"No, I've got it." She's always refused my help, even though I'm capable.

I mean, I learned how to cook from mostly her. Even though Dad also cooked, she used to tell me, in private, his food didn't have enough flavor. When I asked her why she still ate it without adding more, she said because he worked hard on it, and she didn't want to hurt his feelings. Dad has gotten to be a better cook these days because I think he paid attention to her reactions. One day, I want to find someone I'm that in sync with.

"Okay, I can at least set the table."

"That would be helpful." Mom nods in agreement.

I grab three plates out of the cabinet and carry them to the dining room. The table is a long rectangle, but I set them down in the places at the end we usually occupy. I keep asking why they keep such a long table. They like to host some of the holiday gatherings, and that's their reasoning. But honestly, it'd be smarter to get a table that expands when people are over instead of keeping it this big all the time. It just takes up too much space when it's only them ninety percent of the time. It doesn't take long for me to grab the cups and everything else we need at the table.

Dad joins me in the dining room, his hair still wet

causing his short hair to curl on the ends. I'd love to have any of that curl in my hair, but I look more like my mom and got her straight dark hair.

"How are you?" He wraps me in one of the hugs he used to give me as a kid.

Why are my parents acting so strange? My favorite meal and being more affectionate than usual? Something is up. I can't figure out what it is, though.

"I'm good. Thank you for rescheduling dinner to earlier this week. We'll be in full on wedding prep for the rest of the week."

"No problem. It's nice that you still come to these dinners. I can't imagine what it'd be like to not see you regularly, especially if you lived in a different town. Me and Mom cherish these nights."

Okay...maybe nothing is going on. They could be in their feels for other reasons. I'm not sure what, but I'm sure I'll know before the night is over.

Mom carries the pot of picadillo and sets it on trivet she keeps on the table before disappearing into the kitchen again. Next is the warmer for the tortillas. Finally, she grabs a pitcher of sweet tea from the fridge and sets it down on the table.

"Thank you, Mom. It smells delicious."

"You're welcome. We wanted to make tonight special for you."

"Why? This wedding is no different than any of the other ones."

"Yes, it is," Dad says. "It's been publicized heavily, which makes it very different."

Mom keeps checking the watch on her wrist, and it's

odd because she's never done that unless she's expecting something.

"Is everything okay?"

"Of course." She smiles, but it's forced and I need to know what she's hiding.

She holds her hand out for our plates so she can serve our meal. I used to argue with her about doing this, but it brings her joy. Who am I to steal that?

We're about to dig in when there's a knock at the door. "Who's here?"

Mom rushes to the kitchen and brings out another set of dishes.

"Mom?"

Dad leaves the table to answer the door.

"Mom, what did you do?"

When Dad returns moments later, he's not alone. A man I've never seen before stands beside him.

"Emily, this is Dan." Mom makes the introduction.

"Hi." I wave at him before turning to my mother. "Can I speak to you in the kitchen?"

She leads the way to the kitchen and I walk past her to the far side of the room. Our guest does not need to hear this conversation.

"Mom, what are you doing?"

"You said you needed a date to the wedding. Dan is a nice boy, and I think he'd make a good date for you."

"You cannot keep interfering with my life."

"We just want you to be happy, sweetheart." I turn at the sound of Dad's voice. Of course he was in on this.

"I don't need y'all setting me up on dates." I throw my hands in the air. The only way to get them to stop pushing someone on me is if I tell them I have a date. "I already have someone going with me to the wedding."

"Who?" Dad demands.

"Alex." I don't sugarcoat anything. I glare at my father as his face turns a bright shade of red. I should have known something was up as soon as I saw what Mom cooked. "You won't talk me out of it."

"Just give Dan a chance," Mom says.

"No, Mom. I'm a grown woman, and fully capable of choosing my own dates. Thank both of you for your support over the years, but this isn't something you get to have a decision over. Tell Dan, I had an emergency and had to leave."

Instead of letting them talk me out of leaving. I pick up my bag from where I left it on the counter and leave through the back door. I'm tired of this. Now, I need to make sure Alex can go because there's no way I'm going to the wedding alone and letting word get back to my parents.

alex

THE MATERIALS I need for the renovation have started arriving. For now, I've asked Kai if I can store them in the back of the parking lot. I don't want to take up space inside just yet. When I walked inside this morning to double check my measurements, I noticed all the flowers being delivered. The last thing I want to do is take up space while they are busy. We probably should have put off the renovations until after this wedding, but Kai was eager to get started.

"Are you sure you don't need more space?" Emily asks as she arranges the flowers in specific areas.

"The wood outside is fine for now. I brought a tarp to keep in here in case it rains."

"Please don't mention rain." Emily groans. "That's the last thing we need to happen in the next few days."

"Is the wedding outside?"

"Yep, and I fear you've jinxed us." She takes a moment to take stock of her various sections.

She's quiet for a moment. The rigidity of her body,

and head focused solely on the floor means she's got something on her mind. She used to have the same exact stance when she was worried about a test when we were in school.

"Is everything okay? Other than me jinxing the weather?" I take a couple of steps toward her. I know I don't have the right to attempt consoling her, but it doesn't mean I don't want to. If I could take away any pain and frustrations for her, I would in a heartbeat. Not only because I owe it to her, but because I still care for her...even after all these years.

"Yes?" She lifts her hands to her ponytail and pulls it tighter. "No?" Shaking her head she keeps her focus on the flowers.

She opens her mouth to say something and closes it. Then does it a few more times.

"You're gonna catch flies if you keep doing that." Another step, and I'm directly in front of her. There's nowhere for her to look except for at me.

"Sorry." She takes a deep breath and lets it out. Then another one. Now she looks me in the eyes and speaks. "Do you have any plans for Saturday night?"

It's an odd question coming from her given our past. I didn't think she'd want anything to do with me, much less ask about plans. But I know for a fact she has plans.

"Don't you have the wedding Saturday?"

"Yes, and that's why I'm asking."

"I thought you were going stag like Paula."

She grabs the end of her ponytail and plays with it, twirling her hair around her finger. Whatever she's about to say, she doesn't want to. Now her focus is on anything but me.

"My parents tried to set me up with a date to the wedding. We had our weekly dinner last night, and this random guy shows up. They mean well, but give me a break."

"So, they're still trying to give their input on every aspect of your life?" I guess some things never change.

"It's not like that. They care about me is all."

And she's still defending their actions even though it seems to have upset her pretty badly. I wonder if she'd be interested to know how much her dad in particular has interfered in her life. But, I can't do that to her. She'd lose trust in her parents for a long while if she knew they were the ones who pushed me away from her.

"Okay. Why do you need to know if I have plans, this weekend?"

"Um." Her finger twirls faster and faster. "I may have told my parents I was taking you before storming out of their house."

She turns away to hide her embarrassment. That's the last thing she should be feeling. After all these years she's done something to defy what her parents want from her. I remember when they said starting a flower shop with her friends wouldn't be the smartest idea. But they came together with a business plan before they left for college and her parents agreed to fund her degree after seeing it.

It's also interesting she used me as the person she's taking. She has to know they've never really cared for me.

Touching her arm, I turn her back toward me. "You don't have to hide. I'll go with you."

"Really?" She meets my gaze once again. "Oh crap. What about your daughter? I didn't even think about that."

"Don't even worry about it. I'm sure my parents will be fine with watching her."

"Thank you. You have no idea how much this means to me."

I don't think Emily realizes I would do anything for her. Just because I cowered to her dad back then doesn't mean I ever stopped loving her. When we were teens, I always thought we would be end game. But I was young and dumb when I let her dad bully me into breaking up with her. He was terrifying to eighteen year old me.

"No problem. What's the dress code? I don't want to show up looking ridiculous."

"Oh, black tie. I mean, I don't understand why she's doing it that way. It doesn't fit her and Spencer's style, but her cousin, Stella, has had a lot of input with the planning. It's actually going to be on her property."

"That's cool. Where do they live?"

"Oh, you remember that old house down the road from Johnny's? The ones the Garnett's used to own?"

"Yeah."

"That's where Johnny and Stella live."

"That's pretty awesome. I always loved that house. The architecture is beautiful."

Emily rolls her eyes at me. "Always talking about houses. I'm glad that's never changed."

"What can I say? Houses fascinate me."

She laughs and it's the first time since I've been back that her eyes have lit up with joy because of me. It feels good to be the cause of a positive reaction instead of the weary glances she gives me anytime I'm in the shop.

"Is there a specific time I should pick you up?"

"Oh, um, I planned on changing at Stella's since I'll already be there to set up."

"Let me know what time I need to be there, and if anything changes, let me know."

"I will." She takes stock of the groups of boxes and turns toward the door when it opens. The rest of the owners walk in laughing. She steps back, putting a bit more distance between us. "I should get back to work."

"Oh, okay." Interesting she doesn't want her friends to see us talking so closely. I wonder how she's going to explain I'm her date on Saturday. I have a feeling her friends will be shocked, and demanding answers I can't give. The only thing I can do is not read into this more than I should.

The rest of the week has gone off without a hitch. I have almost all of my supplies, and I managed to start working on spaces without getting in the way of the employees. It'll be easier once this wedding is over. At least, that's my hope. Otherwise, this renovation will take ages.

Kira has been running around all over the house.

Mom and Dad got her a small pool to swim in, and she's asking when it'll be ready every five minutes.

I, on the other hand, have been stressing about what I'm going to wear. I know she said it was black tie. I have a tux, but it doesn't fit quite the way I remembered.

"Are you doing okay back here, Son?" Dad's voice booms outside my door.

I feel like I'm eighteen all over again and getting ready for prom. But this time, I'm older and wiser. While Emily's my date, she's not my girlfriend and that feels weird. Now isn't the time to look into that, though.

"Yeah." I turn toward my open door. "Does this look okay?"

"You look fine, Alex." He chuckles. "You know Emily will be happy with whatever you show up in."

"I don't know, Dad. This wedding is a big deal for her business. Everything has to go off without a hitch."

"It will. I've been reading about it online for weeks. Emily and her friends know what they are doing. You just have to show up and be the person on her arm."

"Thanks for putting me at arm candy status."

"Truth hurts, kid."

"Are you sure you and Mom can handle Kira for the night? You know how she gets."

"Honestly, your mom has the whole night planned. I'm in charge of building a fort." My heart swells at the small things Dad will do with her. He worked all the time when I was a kid, and didn't do as much as some of my friends' parents, but building forts in the living room... that was an activity for only us.

"That sounds like fun."

"Are you coming home tonight?" He smirks.

"That's the plan. I'm going as Emily's friend, nothing more."

"Okay." He holds his hands out in surrender and backs down the hallway. "But if anything changes, let us know."

I swear my parents are wanting this to turn into something it's not. At least, I don't think it is. She's using me to get back at her parents, and that's fine by me. It's the perfect amount of pettiness, and I'm happy I can crawl under her dad's skin in this small way. Immature? Definitely. But I don't care. I'll be the one on her arm tonight, and not some random guy her parents know. If I had to guess they picked someone with an office job that doesn't click with Emily in any way possible. They likely thought their guy would be good for Emily's life based on their own thoughts for how it should go.

Enough of that kind of thinking. I won't let her parents ruin my night with her. It may only be for tonight, but I'm okay with it.

My hair is the last thing I check before grabbing my wallet off the bed and heading out of my room. My palms shouldn't be this sweaty when I haven't even made it to the wedding yet.

Kira's eyes widen as soon as I walk into the living room. "Daddy, you look handsome."

"Thank you, pumpkin." I give her a quick hug. "Be good for Grandma and Grandpa. They have a lot of fun planned for you tonight."

"I know." Kira giggles. "Grandma showed me the stuff she got to make friendship bracelets. Even Grandpa is making one."

"Have fun with that." I have a feeling he'll pick out the beads and let mom or Kira string them. He's not exactly graceful with small crafts. That's Mom's area of expertise.

As soon as Kira lets me go, Mom swoops in for a hug. "Have fun tonight. If plans change let us know, and good luck."

Good luck with what? I want to ask her, but if I don't leave soon, I'll be late. The last thing I want is Emily to think I'm standing her up...again.

It doesn't take me long to get to Stella and Johnny's house. Though, I'm surprised there's a long line of cars waiting to pull into the driveway. I didn't realize Tiffany and her soon to be husband are such a big deal. Maybe I should have done some research before agreeing to this.

I inch to the opening of the driveway and I'm stopped by a guy in a security guard uniform. "Name?"

"Oh, um Alex Moody." This feels very official.

The guard looks over the list on his phone and taps the screen. "You're good to go. Follow the line of cars, and a parking attendant will direct you where to park."

"Thanks." Hopefully that came out as a statement and not a question. That guy was intimidating.

After being directed into a parking spot on the edge of the grass, I get out of the car and turn toward the road again. I didn't notice them the first time, but there are a few cars parked haphazardly on the other side. What in the world is going on?

A golf cart is waiting for people to get into the open seats, and I grab the last one, as another approaches to pick up another set of people.

I don't remember this property being so large when I was a kid, but I rarely got the opportunity to come out here. Even back then the Garnetts were an older couple. They came to town events, but for the most part folks left them alone.

Within minutes we're at the house, and I hop off the cart to make my way inside while the other guests walk to the side of the house. Kate is standing at the front door as I approach.

"Alex, what are you doing here? I didn't know you were invited." She wraps me in a hug. She sent me very detailed messages about how she was going to maim me after I broke Emily's heart. But after years, she's let go of that anger.

I take a step back, and admire the woman who used to be one of my closest friends. "Emily invited me as her plus one."

"Oh, why didn't I know that?"

"I have no idea, but ta-da." I wave my hands as if I've just performed a magic trick. "Do you know where I can find her?"

"She's finishing up her hair and makeup. She'll be down in a few minutes. You can wait inside if you want."

"Thanks. We'll find you when she's ready." I push open the door and take a step inside.

People are rushing back and forth, putting last minute finishes on some of the bouquets. I'm not sure where to look for Emily, and I don't want to get in their way. Standing against the wall closest to the door, I wait. She'll come out of one of these rooms eventually.

After a few moments movement from the staircase catches my eye and my jaw drops. I'm never going to survive the night.

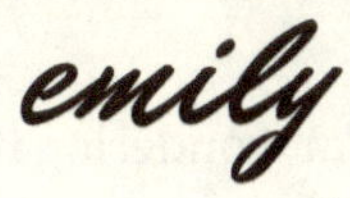

CHAPTER THIRTEEN

IT FEELS like my entire body is sweating. Maybe I should have gone home and had Alex pick me up from there. But we came in the vans from the shop. I didn't want to take one of those in case one of my coworkers needed to run back to the shop for something.

"Are you okay?" Caroline moves behind me, her concern evident in the reflection of the mirror. "You look like you're freaking out a bit. Our job with the flowers is done, and all the arrangements look amazing. Now it's our turn to sit back and relax."

Shaking my head, I stare at the top of the dresser. Stella was kind enough to let us get ready in one of the guest bedrooms. Our Whoopsie Daisy event uniforms are in a pile on the bed. One of us needs to remember to grab those before we leave tonight.

"I'm fine, I think."

"You think?"

"Don't get mad at me for not saying anything earlier, but I invited Alex as my plus one for tonight."

Caroline gasps and I can see all the questions flashing across her face. Luckily, she's not voicing them. There isn't enough time for me question my decision and also explain things.

"You better give me the details on how this happened after the wedding."

"I will, but now I'm wondering if it's a bad idea."

"Why would it be?"

"Because of our past." I know it's futile to still be hung up on that, and it's a poor excuse. "We haven't really talked about it. But we're also getting along really well. It almost feels like old times."

Caroline rubs the top of my shoulders to ease some of the tension that's built there. "Then let it feel like that. I'm not saying forget the past. Both of you are adults now, it's okay for things to feel right between y'all. If things start going South, give me a signal and I'll get you out of here."

"Okay." I take a deep breath and let it out. My phone dings and I grab it off the dresser. "Well, it looks like Kate knows. Alex is waiting for me downstairs."

"You've got this. Let the past stay there and enjoy your night with him. Being excited and nervous doesn't mean it didn't happen. But it does show you're growing and willing to move forward."

"Okay." With one last glance in the mirror, I give myself a mental shake. "Let's do this. Though, I'm blaming all of this on Tiffany. She's the one who insisted we bring dates."

Caroline laughs as she opens the bedroom door and waits for me to walk out. My steps are slow and I make my way out of the room. I can't believe I'm doing this. I should have come alone. Then I wouldn't have all this stress building inside me about how tonight will play out. What happens after the wedding? I didn't even think about that.

"Hold your head up high," Caroline whispers as I cross the threshold. "You are going to make his heart drop."

"Thanks." I square my shoulders and lift my head high. I've never been one to shrink into the crowd even if I'm not the center of attention. And let's be honest, Kate was always the one at the front of the crowd. Tonight, it's my turn to wow the one person I've cared about all these years despite the knife he slid into my heart. Tonight...I'm showing him exactly what he's been missing.

I peek over the staircase and see Alex searching around the room. Moving down the hallway, to the top of the stairs, I take one last breath, and let my feet carry me down the first few steps. I send up small prayers that I won't trip and fall on my face. Heels aren't something I regularly wear, but this occasion needed them.

Before I make it halfway down the stairs, Alex sees me. His eyes wide, and mouth hanging open. It seems I've made an impression.

My heel snags on the stairs as I take the next step and I grab hold of the banister to keep me upright. Don't let this go to your head, Emily. But it's hard not to when he's looking at me as if I'm the only person in the room. I slow my descent. My ability to possibly fall already proven.

Before I realize it, Alex is in front of me, his hand held out for mine. Did he see me stumble and feel like he needs to come to my rescue? Not that I'm not grateful for it. The last thing I want to do is make a mockery of myself before the wedding, and he is keeping me from doing that. Even now, he seems to know exactly what I need.

"You look stunning," he whispers to me as he helps me down the stairs. "Not that you don't any other time I see you, but especially tonight. Watch out, you might upstage the bride."

"That will never happen." I shake my head. Only a few more stairs until we reach the bottom. "Is it just me, or does this feel like when we entered prom? The stair case and awkward stares included."

"Except we're older now and we don't have to spike the punch. I'm sure the booze will be flowing free before the end of the night."

"Oh no doubt. Especially with Crooked Halo in attendance."

"You're kidding." He halts our progress and looks over at me. "They're here? Is that why there was so much fuss to even pull into the driveway?"

"Please don't tell me you're going to fangirl over them. They are normal people just like you and me."

"I can't believe you know them. That's pretty cool. How do the bride and groom know who they are?"

We're back on the move. The wedding starts in ten minutes, and we need to find our seats. "Spencer, the groom, does a lot of their marketing and merchandising. Quite a few people in Asheville know them pretty well now. They stop by from time to time when they don't have any shows. Sometimes they'll play at Out of the Ashes if the mood strikes."

"And nobody here gets starstruck?"

I shrug my shoulders. "Not anymore. At first people were awkward around them, but now they treat them like they are from here."

"Then why all the security up front?"

"To make sure none of their fans from out of town get in. Their attendance is supposed to be a secret. The guards are a precaution."

"Well." Alex clears his throat. "Some folks have definitely found the place. I saw a few cars lined up on the road with people sitting on them."

"And here I was hoping this wedding would go off without a hitch." I groan.

"It's be fine." He reaches over with his free hand and squeezes mine. "Security looked pretty serious. I'm sure they'll handle it."

"You're right." We make our way to the front porch and prepare to walk around. I would have led us to the back porch to find our seats, but that's the direction the wedding party is going. I won't do anything to steal their thunder. "Any particular place you want to sit?"

"I'm the interloper here, I'm fine with wherever you choose."

I'm leading us down the aisle on the bride's side when I see my friends waving their arms at us. "We saved you a seat."

We hurry over to sit down before the ceremony begins. "Thanks," I whisper to my friends.

"No problem." Kate smiles.

"You are definitely going to explain this as soon as we're back at home." Samantha points to me then Alex.

Way to put me on the spot. Alex does his best to keep his head down so I can't see his expression, but I'm almost certain he's enjoying this.

Not one minute after, the music starts and the bridal party makes their way down the aisle. Tiffany kept it small with her cousins as her maids of honor, and their partners are the best men. It's a good thing they all get along or it might be awkward.

Once they are by the arch, the music changes and we all stand. Tiffany is at the end of the aisle. She has a princess style white dress with colors woven into the tulle. She also added butterflies to give it the whimsical look. It's absolutely stunning and she's such a beautiful bride.

As she passes our seats a single tear trickles down my cheek. It never fails, weddings will always make me cry. It hits even more with Alex by my side because when I was younger, I envisioned this moment for us. But it never came.

Alex looks back at me and notices the tear. "Do you need a tissue?"

"No." I wipe my cheek. "I'm good."

"Are you sure?"

"Yeah, don't worry about me."

In less than twenty minutes, we're standing and clapping as Tiffany and Spencer make their way back down the aisle as a married couple. She wasn't playing when she said she was keeping the ceremony short and sweet.

Stella comes back to the archway where there's a microphone. "If everyone can make their way toward the tents, dinner will be served shortly. Feel free to stop by the bar on the way to your table."

"A drink sounds amazing." Kate turns toward the outside of the aisle and makes her way to the tent, Xander trailing behind her.

The rest of us follow suit. I'm pretty sure we're at the same table, and Kate's right, a drink sounds amazing. I'll need something to loosen up for the rest of the night. Being here with Alex has me on high alert. It'll be so easy to fall for him all over again.

Not that I'm not already doing that. Seeing him in the shop almost every day makes it difficult to resist his charm. The wild thing is he doesn't even try. It's who he is. The genuine kindness and willingness to help others is something that's always been a part of him. Which is why it doesn't make sense that he'd dump me so carelessly all those years ago. But I won't focus on that tonight. We can have that conversation some other time.

The DJ starts playing music while the caterers are getting the food set up and Tiffany gets changed for the reception. We've all sat down when Alex turns to me, his hand held out. "Would you like to dance?"

Would I? Yes. But I worry it will blur the boundaries between us. Make tonight seem like more than it is. A petty ploy to piss my parents off, even though I still don't understand why they dislike Alex so much.

I quickly glance at my friends to see what they think.

All four of them are nodding at me. Paula even makes a shooing motion with her hands. For someone who didn't bring a date, she's sure invested in what I'm doing.

Alex's eyes are still on me when I turn back to him. "Yes."

He pulls me from my seat and leads us to the dance floor. There are a few couples hand in hand, making the most of their night out, and waiting for the bride and groom to make their way to the festivities.

The song is slow, and Alex pulls me close to him. My head leaning against his chest as we sway back and forth. This feels right. Like we've done it a hundred times. We did back in high school at all the formal dances, and those feelings of happiness flood into me. The only difference...he's a much better dancer than he was back then.

"Are you having fun tonight?" His voice sends shivers across my skin.

"Actually, yeah." I nod against him. "I'm not used to coming to client's weddings, but I'm enjoying the evening. Thank you for coming with me."

"No, the pleasure is all mine." He pushes me out into a spin before pulling me back to him. "You took my breath away the moment I saw you tonight."

I feel like he wants to say more, but he leaves it there.

"Thank you." It's been so long since I've been complimented by someone. The fact it's coming from him makes it all the more special.

"I mean it." His fingers circle at the small of my back, and I want nothing more than to melt into him. To spend the rest of the night wrapped in his arms, the past be damned. He's clearly grown up in the ten plus years we've been apart.

"I've never doubted your words. You aren't one to say things you don't mean."

"Not always." He sighs. I can't help but wonder what he's talking about because I have a feeling it's something in regards to me.

"What do you mean?"

"This isn't the time or place." He pulls me closer to him. It feels like he'll never let me go again, and I'm not sure I'd want him to.

CHAPTER FOURTEEN

EMILY'S BODY close to mine is all I've ever wanted. It's no different than when we were fifteen and dating in high school. Now, though, we have experience and wisdom on our side. We're capable of making decisions without giving a damn what other people think, or have to say.

Her words echo in my head, and the shame that comes with them hits me in the gut. There's only one time I've said what I didn't mean, and that was at her father's insistence. I can't tell her he's the reason, though. It would destroy the relationship she has with her parents and I wouldn't wish that on anyone. I know what it's like to be pulled away from your family because of the person you're with.

The song changes to something fast paced and Emily leads me off the dance floor back to our seats. "Thanks."

"For what?"

"The dance."

"You're welcome."

If I can do anything that puts that gorgeous smile and serene look on her face, I'll do it. If for nothing else than to make up for the shitty way I treated her our freshman year of college. She deserved better than that, and maybe, if things go well tonight, I can make that right.

"Has anyone told y'all how cute you are together?" Paula claps her hands.

"Every day since they dated in high school." Samantha groans. "At every function, or dance, they were in their own little world."

"Oh, I didn't know that." Paula's cheeks turn a light shade of pink. "If you aren't still dating, maybe you should give it another shot."

Emily reaches for the napkin on the table and fiddles with edge. Keeping herself distracted from the suggestion. I'd kill to know what's going on in her brain right now.

To Paula, I say, "I'd be game for giving it another go."

Our friend group gasps at my declaration. Clearly, they didn't think I'd go there. Tonight feels magical, though. Anything can happen. As long as Emily can keep an open mind about me, I'll take it.

Our conversation is interrupted when the DJ announces the newly wedded couple. Everyone stands as they make their way to the center of the dance floor and embrace each other as a love song plays over the speakers.

They truly look happy. I don't even know this couple, aside from the brief interaction with Tiffany, but you can tell how much they love each other.

I watch the two of them twirl around the dance floor. Only stopping to start the next dance between Tiffany and her father. Then one more time when Spencer hits the floor with his mom.

This could have been me and Emily. There's a slim chance it could still be our future, but not for a very long time. Not until I can prove myself to her.

Once the dances are over, the DJ announces food will be served. The bridal party and parents will go first, then everyone else can line up.

Tiffany must not have heard him, or she doesn't care, because she makes a beeline for our table. "The arrangements are beautiful and everything I imagined. Thank y'all so much."

All of the Whoopsie Daisy employees say "thank you" in unison. It's a little weird how in sync they are sometimes. I guess that's what comes from over thirty years of friendship.

Tiffany catches sight of me and grins. "I see you brought a date after all, Emily. I hope the two of you booze up and have a blast tonight."

Instead of answering, Emily buries her head in her arms on the table. Her hair swaying back and forth as she shakes her head. "I swear that woman will be the death of me," her voice is a soft mumble.

"Why's that?"

"Because she knew I was bringing you." She lifts her head and stares at the lights covering the tent ceiling. "She had to add your name to the guest list."

"She's only teasing you." Kate laughs. "But the look on your face was worth it."

"Shut up." Emily grabs a leaf that fell to the table and throws it at her friend. "I'm glad I can bring all of you so much amusement."

I've been around one of their arguments before. It can go one of two ways; fizzles out to nothing, or they won't speak to each other for the rest of the night.

Grabbing Emily's hand, I stand. "Maybe we should get in line for food."

"That sounds like a fantastic idea." She sticks her tongue out at her friends and follows me to the table. "Sorry about them. I hope they aren't making you feel uncomfortable."

"Please," I scoff. "We've said and done worse to each other growing up. It's going to take a lot more than small remarks to run me off."

"Oh, so you're planning on sticking around?" She grins up at me.

"I mean, my kid does go to school here and we've been looking for a place to live." I cock my head to the side. "I'd say that's a pretty solid answer that we're sticking around."

"That's not what I meant and you know it." She smacks my stomach with the back of her hand.

"As long as I'm still accepted in the friend group, then I'm here to stay." I kiss the top of her head before taking a step forward in the line. Her body melts into mine and I know I've said the right words.

After getting our plates we head back to the table. Nobody is there except Paula, and someone I don't know. Which isn't odd considering I haven't been home for a while. New people move to small towns all the time.

"Are we interrupting?" Emily asks as we take our seats.

"Not at all." Paula smiles. "He was just leaving."

The man next to her doesn't move for a second, and I hope he's not being a jerk. Finally, he stands and walks away from the table. But none of us miss the way he turns back to get one last look at Paula.

"I feel like I've seen him somewhere," Emily mutters under her breath. She takes a drink of the water in front of her and her eyes widen. "Oh my God. He's with Crooked Halo."

Paula groans. "He's part of the crew."

"I didn't realize there was anything going on between you. Is that why you've kept quiet about where you go at lunch?"

"Hell no." Paula laughs. "That's for something else entirely. I think I'm gonna get some food."

As soon as Paula leaves the table, Emily shakes her head. "One of these days I'll figure out what she doesn't want us to know."

"Or, you can wait for her to tell you."

The glare Emily shoots in my direction is enough to know I've said the wrong thing. I swear the four of them feel like they need to know what everyone in their circle is up to at all times. The lack of secrets is probably why they work so well together, but it can seem weird to outsiders.

Emily takes a few bites of her food before clearing her throat and turning her attention to me. "Do you have to be home at certain time for Kira?"

I think back to my parents telling me not to worry

about her. They want me to enjoy the evening, especially since I'm spending it with Emily. They've always loved her like a daughter and I got so much crap from them when they found out I broke up with her.

"Nope. My parents have an entire evening of fun planned out for her, including making friendship bracelets."

"That sounds like a giant mess." She laughs, and God how I've missed it.

"It probably will be. I'm sure we'll be vacuuming beads for at least a month after this." I place my hand over hers and give it a gentle squeeze. "Why do you ask?"

"Just wondering."

"There's never a reason for you just wonder." I poke her in her side and she jumps.

"You still freaking do that?" When I nod and grin she shakes her head. "I'll have to be on high alert from now on. You know how ticklish I am."

"You're avoiding the question."

"Fine." She huffs. "Would you maybe want to come over after the wedding festivities are over? We can catch up and talk without everyone around."

Finally, the question I've been wanting her to ask since the evening began. She glances at our hands. Mine over hers until she turns her around and clasps them together.

"Absolutely." It takes everything in me not to throw my free hand up in victory. "The only rule is I have to be home before Kira wakes up. She does this thing where she busts through the door for a wakeup call."

"Nobody said you were staying the night." She smirks.

I lift my hands in surrender. "I was only letting you know in case we lose track of time."

Presumptuous of me? Probably. But I want to spend as much time with her tonight as I can. Who knows when we'll be able to do it again.

***

The drive to Emily's house doesn't take as long as I thought it would. But, we also left way before everyone else, as they wanted to see Tiffany and Spencer cut the cake, Emily was ready to go.

"I didn't realize you lived this close to the shop."

"It's easier for me to be close." Emily shrugs as she unbuckles her seatbelt. "Anytime there's a problem, I'm the one they call."

"That makes sense, though I don't know why they would only call you."

"Because they can't understand my organization system for some reason." She shakes her head as I get out of the car to open her door. "I even have it written down on a piece of paper in the office."

"Not everyone is as serious about keeping files a certain way as you, Em."

"They should be." She laughs and leads the way to her door. "Kai tried coming up with his own system for the office once, and I couldn't find anything. He's probably the only one who understands it. But he hasn't been here since the beginning."

"Yeah, he told me about that." I wait behind her wondering if she's ever brought anyone else home. It's none of my business and I'm sure she's dated people since we broke up, but the thought wiggles in the back of my head. "You have no idea how grateful he is about y'all giving him a chance."

"Oh, we know." Emily turns the key in the lock and swings the door open. "He's constantly buying us coffee or breakfast. He acts like he's the only person we've hire in recent months."

"I thought you had the same group of people for a while. From I can tell, y'all work like you've known each other for years."

"Nope. We didn't start getting a ton of business until Tiffany and Spencer said they were using us for the flower arrangements."

"How did people even know that?" It's weird they'd make that announcement when they aren't even the celebrities.

"Tiffany mentioned it to a fan at the merch booth during one of the shows and word spread like wildfire." Emily grabs hold of the wall as she slips out of her heels and I shut the door. "They may not be a part of the band, but the fans love them just the same."

Okay, that makes sense. From the few interactions I've had with Tiffany, she definitely has charisma. There's no doubt the Crooked Halo fans feed off that. Add in the fact her and Spencer are polar opposites and they are a match made in indie alternative heaven.

"Well, I'm glad it brought you more business. Y'all are doing well for yourselves."

"Yeah, and now that Tiff's wedding is over, we can breathe a bit."

"Won't more people book you after they see the photos?"

"Probably, but until that happens, I'm going to relax and handle the small weddings we have over the next few months."

"That's smart."

She leads me to the living room and disappears into the kitchen for a few moments. My favorite beer is in each hand as she makes her way toward the couch.

"Here you go." She hands me one.

"Were you expecting me to come over all along?"

"No." She snorts. "I also happen to like this beer." She takes a drink and sets it down on the coffee table in front of us. "So, what's been going on with you? What led you back to Asheville?"

I'm not certain she wants to open that can of worms.

CHAPTER FIFTEEN

THE HOUSE IS SILENT. I wish I would have had the forethought to put some music on when we got here. Doing it now feels like I'm trying to cover up the awkwardness between us.

Alex is peeling at the edges of the label on his bottle. I'm not sure if he's trying to think through what he wants to tell me, or if he wants to spare my feelings about everything that happened. Either way, I'll give him time to collect his thoughts. There's no way in hell I plan on ruining the night by demanding answers to questions he may not be ready to give me.

"I don't even know where to start."

"The beginning?"

"Well, once up on a time two people fell in love."

"You know what I mean, smart ass." I tap his knee with my foot.

"Yeah, yeah."

He grabs my foot and rubbing me feet. Normally anything to do with feet grosses me out, but this feels...

heavenly. And very intimate, but I'm not going to stop him. Not if it will help him give me some insight into the person he is now.

"Let's see, I made one of the biggest mistakes of my life. Got my degree. Then I met someone, got married and started my own company. The second biggest mistake. Not the company, but marrying her. The only good thing I got out of that was Kira."

He pauses in massaging my foot for a moment, gathering his thoughts. I don't say anything out of fear he'll stop talking.

"When things got hard and Kira wouldn't be the little girl, she wanted her to be, she split. Signed over her rights, and I've had her ever since. But it's hard running your own business with the hours I have while taking care of kid. I thought it would be best if I came home. At least I have a support system here. And that's pretty much it."

"Sounds like life threw you some curveballs." I almost pull my foot out his hand because the action seems to light for such a heavy admission. I want to ask him what the biggest mistake was. I have a feeling it has to do with me, but I don't want to press the issue.

"You could say that." He shrugs. "I'm not upset about it, though. It led me back to you. Kira wasn't lying, you know."

"About what?"

"The pictures I have of us in my closet. Even though I made a dumbass decision, I never stopped loving you. If I could go back and do it over again, I never would have broken up with you."

"Don't say that." This time I do pull my foot from his hands. I slide over until I'm sitting next to him, our legs touching with no space between us. "Things happen the way they do for a reason. If you hadn't gone off on your own side quest, you would have never had Kira. And from the few minutes I spent with her, I know she's an amazing girl."

"Amazing and terrifying all at the same time."

"I can believe that." The room goes quiet once again. He's shared his life, and now I want to share something with him as well. Even though he still hasn't told me why he broke up with me, this feels like a moment for honesty. "I compared every guy I dated to you. It's most likely why I'm still single. Nobody could live up to the space you have in my heart. No matter how much I tried to get over you. I couldn't."

He doesn't hesitate. His hands cup my face and his lips crash into mine. All the pent-up emotions. The chemistry between us that doesn't seem to go away. All of that has led to this moment. Putty in each other's hands because despite whatever bullshit we've been through, we came back to each other.

His lips leave mine and I whimper at the loss. Leaning his forehead against mine, he takes a few breaths. "I'm sorry. I should have asked if that was even okay."

"You didn't see me stopping you, did you?"

He shakes his head. "No."

Lifting my dress, I climb into his lap and wrap my arms around him. "Then don't."

Now that I've said the words out loud, he doesn't

hold back. Our lips meet once again. His tongue slipping into my mouth to dance with my own. His hands on my butt pulling me against him, creating friction between us in the best possible way.

This is the passion I've longed for all these years, knowing damn well there's only one person who can create fireworks with me. Running my fingers through his hair, I deepen the kiss. I'm doing everything I can to let him know just how much I've missed him despite the different paths our lives took.

His fingers trace a line down my lower back and I giggle at the contact. I can fill his lips turn up into a smirk before he changes direction and his fingers trail down my thigh to the edge of my dress. His hand slips underneath and the friction of the calluses on his fingers against my smooth skin makes me shiver.

He pulls back. "Are you okay?"

"Yes," I gasp before placing kisses along his jawbone.

His lips caress my neck before landing on my earlobe. A tiny nibble, as his fingers push aside my panties and slip inside of me. My breaths are quick as I ride his hand while he sucks on my earlobe. The one spot he knows will turn me into putty in his hands.

He moves his other hand from my butt and I feel it tightening around the loose tendrils of my hair. Before long I'm seeing stars and his grip tightens as I throw my head back in ecstasy.

Letting go of my hair, he positions his hand on my back before removing his other hand from under my dress. He lays me on the couch and reaches in his back pocket. Retrieving a foil packet, he throws his wallet to the floor. I can see how much wants me by the bulge in his dress pants. They don't leave much to the imagination.

"I can stop if you want me to." He says as he rips open the condom packaging. "This is probably too fast for either of us."

"I don't want you to stop, Alex. I want you...now."

Without a word he kicks off his shoes, unbuttons his pants and shoves them down his legs along with his boxers. As he rolls on the condom, he smirks at me. "The only thing that would be hotter is if you still had your heels on. It would be like recreating graduation night."

"Later." I groan at the sight of him. "We'll relive that night some other time. But right now, I need you."

"You've got it."

He wastes no time pulling my panties off and sliding my dress to my waist before plunging into me. His grip tight on my hips and my legs wrapped around him, pulling him deeper into me. We can have fun with foreplay later. The pent up need inside of both us has come to its boiling point. Tonight, we are raw and emotional. Showing each other how much we've yearned for each other despite the time, distance, and grievances.

My body will hate me tomorrow for being on this tiny sofa, but all the matters to me is this moment with Alex. He leans down and takes my bottom lip between his, sucking on it as my fingers dig into his back. It doesn't take long before I lose control once again. This time he follows along after me.

We stare at each other a few moments before he

shifts from on top of me to beside me. "That was... intense."

"Yeah." I'm doing the best I can to catch my breath. "It was."

"Any chance you have a large pair of sweats I can change into? I know I look hot in my suit, but I think the rest of the night calls for something a little more comfortable."

My cheeks redden before I say the words. "I actually have some of yours from when you visited me in college."

"Seriously?" His chuckle vibrates against my neck. "You have them after all this time. I thought I lost them."

"What?" I laugh. "They're comfy. Let me grab them for you."

I slide off the couch and grab my panties from the floor before heading to the room. Alex is following along after me with his pants balled up in front of him. As if I've never seen him naked and we didn't just have sex. "Um, where's the restroom?"

Crap. I forgot to give him a tour of the house. "There's one down the hall to the left, or you can use the one in my room."

"I'll go to this one." He jerks his thumb over his shoulder toward the hall. "I'll grab the clothes when I'm done."

A part of me wonders if he's regretting what happened, but the larger part of me thinks he needs compose himself. I know I do after being sprawled out on my sofa.

I pull out the top drawer of my dresser and grab his old sweats and a t-shirt. It might be odd that I've kept them after all these years, but I don't care. They really are comfortable and they reminded me of him when I'd let myself think of what could have been. Looks, like it was a good idea after all.

Setting them on the bed, I reach back into the drawer for my jammies and head to the bathroom attached to my room. After spending all day in the heat, I need a shower. That, however, takes away from time with Alex and I want that more than the shower.

The clothes are gone when I walk out of the bathroom, but Alex is nowhere in sight. For a second, I think he left without saying anything, but I hear pops coming from the front of the house. What in the hell is he doing?

As I round the corner, I spot him in the kitchen standing close to the microwave. The gentle hum broken up by popping kernels. His focus is solely on the machine.

"What are you doing?"

He jumps back a foot and then glares at me. "Shhh, I'm making sure I don't burn the popcorn."

"The microwave has a timer."

"Those suck. You have to listen to the popcorn."

Okay, he's officially lost it. I always use the timer and my popcorn has never been burnt. To each their own, I guess. I leave him to his devices and move toward the living room, picking up the remote and turning on the TV. "Anything in particular you want to watch?"

When he doesn't say anything, I glance over at the kitchen. He's mouthing numbers between each pop. "Done." He pushes the button and the door swings open. After he pours the contents of the bag into a bowl, he holds it out as an offering. "Perfectly prepared popcorn."

"I see. What's the magic number?"

"Three." He stops by the fridge to grab two fresh beers from the fridge and makes his way toward me. "When you hear three seconds between each pop, it's time to take it out."

I grab a few pieces and put them in my mouth. So, his popcorn is better that mine. I'll never tell him, though. "It tastes the same as mine."

"It's okay, you don't have to admit it. Just know that I know." He taps his head before pulling me closer and setting the bowl in his lap. "One day you'll admit it."

This night truly has been one of the best nights I've had in a long time, from beginning to end. But I think my favorite part is how he's made himself at home in my space. It's like we've picked up where we left off and all's right with the world. I only hope our mad dash to spend time together doesn't end up in a crash scene.

A NOISE WAKES ME UP. It takes me a moment to realize I'm not in my bed and Kira hasn't jumped on me this morning. My left arm feels heavy and numb. Peeling my eyes open, I realize it's Emily snuggled up against me. Her slow breaths not registering the sound coming from across the room. She must have been exhausted after everything yesterday. I know she was at the house long before any of the guests arrived.

Oh shit, that's my ringtone. I slowly slide my arm from under Emily, ignoring the tingles with every movement. Waking her up isn't an option when she so clearly needs the rest. Now that I'm free, I slide out of the bed and tiptoe to my crumpled up pants.

Mom's name flashes across the screen and I silence the call before stepping outside of the room. The door clicks shut behind me as I try not to disturb Em.

As soon as I'm away from the door, I press my mom's number and call her back. "Is everything okay? What time is it?"

"I guess you lost track of time." Mom laughs on the other end. "It's almost ten."

"Shit. Is Kira awake?"

"Yep. She's been awake for about thirty minutes."

Groaning, I wipe a hand down my face. "Please tell me she hasn't been to my room yet."

"Oh, she definitely has. When she asked me where you were, I told her you left to get donuts since she was so good for us last night."

At least that buys me a bit of time, except now I have to come home with donuts. I feel like mom had this excuse in holding for a while.

"I'll be there as soon as I can." I glance around the living room for my keys and wallet. Both are sitting on the coffee table, right where I left them.

"Take your time, honey," Mom says. I can hear Kira giggling in the background. I'm sure Dad is keeping her occupied while Mom fills me on what I need to do. "We've got her. It's not like she's staring at the clock waiting for you to walk through the door. She has no concept of time like her grandpa."

"Yes, I do," I hear Dad yell.

"Okay." It's a slight relief that Kira doesn't seem to be missing me too much right now. Though it stings a bit since before we came to Asheville, it was only me and her against the world. But I'd like Emily to become a part of that as well. "I'll see you in a bit."

"Remember, there's no rush."

"Bye, Mom." Rolling my eyes I tap the end call button and set my phone next to my wallet.

Arms wrap around my shoulders and Emily rests her head against me. "Is everything alright?"

"Yeah, Kira's awake."

"Damn." She gives my shoulders a small squeeze. "I completely forgot to set my alarm last night to wake you up. I'm so sorry."

"It's not a big deal, I promise."

She shakes her head and takes her arms off me, and I miss the contact as soon as she does. "But it is. She expected you to be in your bed, and you weren't because you're here. I don't want to be the cause of any disappointment with Kira."

Nope, there will be none of that. I lift her off the couch and pull her into my lap. "You aren't causing any rifts between me and Kira. Both of you are important to me."

"But you said she was awake and she always goes to your room as soon as she gets up."

"She does." I nod my confirmation. "But my mom told her I was out getting donuts. She won't expect me for a bit."

"It doesn't take that long to get donuts."

"Would you quit trying to think of reasons to push me out the door. Mom told me there's no rush." I nip at her bottom lip and she melts against me.

It doesn't last long because she jerks away and eyes me. "I don't think this is what your mom had in mind when she said you didn't have to hurry back."

"Clearly you don't know how badly she wants us to get back together." I pull her back to me. "I can almost guarantee you this is exactly what she meant."

"Oh my gosh." She buries her head in my chest. "There's no way we're having sex with your mom's blessing. That's weird. Also, who said anything about getting back together?"

"If you think I'm going to let you get away from me again, you're wrong." I lift her up and carry her to her bed. "There's no way in hell I'm going to ruin a second chance with you."

"Well, when you put it like that." She giggles as my fingers slide against her sides to pull her shirt over her head. I could get used to starting my mornings like this.

※

Kira is sitting at the table playing a board game with my parents when I walk in. A box of donuts in one hand and tray with three coffees in the other. I have a feeling we'll all need it to handle Kira's energy.

"Daddy," Kira yells as soon as she sees me. "We had so much fun last night."

"I'm happy, kiddo." I set the donuts and coffee on the bar before she topples me over. "What are you doing now?"

"A Monopoly rematch with Grandpa."

"She cheats," Dad grunts from the table. "I don't understand how she always ends up with all the money."

"No, she doesn't." I shake my head as I set her down. "She knows how to strategize." I walk over to the table and check out the current game. "Why don't you own any property?"

"Because I keep landing on all the crappy ones."

"Never underestimate the profit on even the smallest properties."

"So, you're the reason she keeps beating me. I figured she'd go easy on me since I'm her grandpa."

I can't help the laugh that busts through. "Not a chance. She's more competitive than me and my friends ever were."

"Speaking of friends." Dad winks at me. "How did last night go?"

Of course, he would ask about that right now. Even though it's not a completely appropriate conversation to have in front of Kira. At least, not until I know for sure what's going on with me and Emily. She didn't exactly object when I said I wasn't letting her go this time. But that doesn't mean she's willing to be exclusive after one night. I'll just have to play my cards right to show her I'm not the boy I was back then.

"Last night was...developmental." It's the best way I can think to put it in terms where dad will understand and Kira won't. It'll be nice when I can talk about Emily in front of her. Actually, after I figure out what's going on between the two of us, I should have a talk with Kira about seeing her.

"I hope that means good news is on the horizon."

"What good news?" Mom asks as she comes to the table with a stack of napkins.

"Oh my gosh, guys." I run a hand through my hair. "There isn't any sort of news right now. Except for the fact that I have everything I need to start the renovation."

"Oh, well that's wonderful," Mom says she places the

napkins on the table. "I've heard of so many people having delays in their building projects because they couldn't get the materials."

"That's not the news I was talking about." Dad rolls his eyes.

Mom stares at the both of us for a second before her eyes widen. She gasps, "Oh. That is exciting news."

"Don't get your hopes up. I don't know if there's anything to report on that front yet." But when I do Kira will be the first to know.

"Honestly." Mom laughs. "I'd be surprised if we don't know before even you do."

"Why do you say that?"

"Did you forget we live in Asheville. There is a whole group of little old ladies who hang out at Out of the Ashes for lunch every day and spread the town gossip."

I glance over at her. "Are you one of these ladies?"

"No, of course not." Mom shakes her head. "I just happen to be friends with some of them. Besides, I'm much too busy having fun with Kira to go have lunch."

I swear this town is going to be the death of me. While I love all the reasons I moved here with Kira, being part of the town gossip mill is one of the reasons I was so happy when I left. Too bad it's not something I can control. Otherwise, nobody would know anything about what happens between me and Emily unless we want them to. Although I'm almost certain she's getting the same treatment from her friends as we speak.

"What are we doing today daddy?" Kira asks as she rolls the dice and takes a bite of her donut.

"I'm not sure. I thought maybe we could practice a little bit."

"Really?" She bounces up and down. "Can one of my friends come over to practice with me?"

I glance at Mom and Dad. She's never asked for friends to come over. Both of them nod. If they say it's a good idea, then why not. It'll be good for her to see her friends during the summer.

"Sure, if it's okay with her parents."

"Good because we both need to practice. We're the youngest ones on the team."

She's being melodramatic about the age thing, but they're only the youngest by a couple of months. A lot of the time I think she's being too hard on herself. She barely started playing softball, and shouldn't expect herself to be perfect a couple of months in.

Now's not the time to start that argument though. It would ruin the whole vibe of the morning, and so far, it's been pretty fantastic. I was able to wake up next to the woman I've thought about for years, and my family is rooting for me. Today feels like I won the lottery.

"After we practice maybe we can grab a pizza or something for dinner. Give Grandma night off from cooking."

Mom scoffs. "More like give your dad and night off. It was his turn to man the grill."

Of course I'd pick the night he's cooking to get pizza.

"Just look at it as shifting responsibilities." I grin. "Dad can grill tomorrow night."

"Dang it," he mutters under his breath. "I guess that's fine with me."

He doesn't have much of a choice because we're getting pizza tonight. It won't kill him to cook tomorrow instead. It's part of the perks of being a Dad. Maybe we should put a calendar on the wall with days people have dinner duty.

Although it'll be much easier getting Kira on a schedule when we have a place of our own. I really need to move that up the to do list. As much as I love my parents and how much we get along, this isn't exactly the best place to be bringing people home without Kira knowing.

Not that it's the only thing I'm looking for with Emily, but it's bound to happen. It's something I'll have to worry about later.

For now, I'm going to enjoy the fact that Emily spent hours with me, and that my baby girl is excited to see me because a lot of parents don't have that. As bad as things have been and could be, it's these small moments of joy I try to focus on.

As far as I'm concerned, the only way to go from here is up. I feel like nothing can knock me down.

CHAPTER SEVENTEEN

MY FRIENDS ARE like ping pong balls bouncing around with all the questions they're asking. You would think we could hold off on this conversation until Monday, when I see them at work. But no, they want to discuss it...now. They want all the details of how everything went down. Too bad I'm not ready to give them those details yet.

"Come on," Kate whines. "You have to give us something. Y'all left the wedding pretty early compared to the rest of us."

"Actually, no, I don't." I finish arranging the plate of cheese and crackers. I'm glad I had some on hand when they gathered outside my door thirty minutes ago. They couldn't even give me a day. What if Alex had still been here? What am I saying? They still wouldn't care.

They aren't used to me being the one that says no when it comes to the goings on in our lives. Even Paula is sitting in my living room, and she's never tag teamed me with the rest of the group. She typically stays in her own little bubble unless we're at work or the occasional girls' night when she can make it.

"You know that isn't fair, right?" Samantha huffs. "You always get the details when one of us falls hopelessly in love. So why don't you spill?"

Am I hopelessly in love? I don't think so, not after one night, despite the fact we were together before. But I wasn't lying last night when I told him I still loved him, and I always have. Probably always will, no matter what happens. He was my first love, and while that sounds cliche, I'm okay with that.

He truly understood me better than anybody else, and never made fun of me for my organization, being kind hearted, or thinking through most of the problems I faced. Unlike the rest of my friends. Even when Caroline was going through crap with her now ex-husband, I never once tried to sway her opinion one way or the other. And this was back in high school when we all hated him. That feeling never changed, even when he pulled her away from us.

But this is different. We're too new for there to be any gossip to spread or emotions to spill. And although I think we've got into a monogamous relationship last night, at least, that's what I assume, after his declaration. I didn't correct him. I'm willing to give it a shot if he is. I should probably make sure we're on the same page. Last night wasn't just a fling of passion.

At least I know that he won't have Kira's mom coming back into the picture trying to start up drama since she signed her rights away. Right now, I think the biggest obstacle is getting my parents to like him and find out why they don't, because he really is a good guy. A great father and a pretty awesome friend when you need one, unless you're bleeding.

When I'm done arranging the tray again, I glance up. Four pairs of eyes are on me. I guess I spaced out with all the thoughts running through mind.

"Did y'all get the vans unpacked?" I ask, as my friends glare at me.

"I don't think so." Kate slaps her hand on the table. "You're not getting out of this. Stop trying to dodge the question."

Wow. I don't think I've ever seen her get mad because I wouldn't tell her anything before. I guess it makes sense because not only does Alex affect me, he's also intertwined in the business for a moment.

"Alright, alright. He brought me home last night, and he stayed the night."

"And?" Kate asks.

"And I'm not giving you the gritty details of what we did all night. When have I ever been one to kiss and tell?"

"Oh, you were up all night?" Kate wiggles her eyebrows up and down. She looks ridiculous, but she's not upset anymore.

"So, are y'all like a couple now?" Paula asks as she makes herself a small cheese sandwich.

"I think so." I shrug. "I'm not exactly sure."

"How aren't you sure if you're a couple?" Caroline pipes in before taking a drink of her sweet tea. "Isn't that the first thing you're supposed to establish?"

"What? Like you and Carlos did?" I argue.

"That was a completely different circumstance. We were dealing with my asshole ex-husband."

"He mentioned something about not letting go of me again, which is why I think we're a couple. Am I reading too much into it?"

"Nope." Paula shakes her head. "You're definitely in a relationship now. You might want to make sure, though."

"Probably." As much as they drive me bananas, I'm glad they are here. Even if they are peppering me with questions about Alex. "For real, though, who got the vans back to the shop and unloaded them?"

Kate waves away my concern. "Xander took care of it."

"By himself?" There's no way. I mean, we didn't have to bring much back, but it's still a lot for one person.

"Ben helped," Sam adds.

"So did Carlos," Caroline offers.

"Only one of them is even an employee." I throw my hands in the air.

"They wanted to give us the day off since we've been working so hard. Let them do the work."

"Okay." I hold my hands up in surrender. It is thoughtful of them to step in for us. We have been pushing ourselves more than usual. "Is anyone else hungry?"

"You have cheese." Paula points to the tray. "Is that not enough?"

"Absolutely not." Kate jumps up. "I can grab food."

Honestly, I need a break from them being nosey. "It's okay. I can go."

"Are you sure?" Caroline asks.

"Absolutely. I think I'm in the mood for pizza."

"Oh, don't forget garlic bread and dipping sauce." Sam grabs a piece of cheese. "You are going to the place on the square, right?"

"As if I'd go anywhere else." Sometimes it's like they don't even know me. As someone who relies on folks to shop small, I do the same. It's the only way we can keep our town alive and growing. "I'll be right back. I'll stop and get some wine, too."

Standing, I head toward the door and grab my keys. My friends are cheering behind me. Most likely because of the wine. I just need some time to think.

***

I probably should have called ahead with the order. The restaurant isn't busy, but they make the food fresh right when you order it, so it takes a bit. Pulling my phone out of my pocket, I sit down on one of the chairs by the door. Even though I know I shouldn't look for pictures of the wedding just yet, I need to know if people have posted. Mostly, I want to know if they liked the floral arrangements. Selfish? A little. I already know they are going to get love from the Crooked Halo fans, but I need to see our work.

Trying to stop my finger from tapping the social media icon is futile. A post from Tiffany is the first one to show up. It's a candid picture of her and Spencer. If I had to guess, Stella probably took it. The two of them are so ridiculously in love. Double tapping the screen to like it, I scroll down. There's a notification at the top of the screen, and I check to see what it is.

Tiffany tagged me in a post. Let's see what it is. It's a picture of our group at our table laughing. I wish I knew what we were laughing about. Alex's arm is around my chair and I'm leaning into him. My heart flutters looking at it. The photo is reminiscent of our high school days when none of us went anywhere without the group. The only difference is we've added on to our little family.

She's added more photos this post with shots of our arrangements and also tagged the shop. There are over a hundred comments beneath and I'm terrified to look at them. What if they hate them? Deep breath in and out. I click the comment button and hope for the best.

From the first few comments, it seems like everyone loves them which is a huge plus. I'm sure our inbox will be full of orders when we get to the shop in the morning. I keep scrolling and pull my thumb away once I recognize the names of the some of the commenters. They are people from Asheville. People we went to school with.

It looks like someone rekindled their high school romance.

The whole gang is back together. Here comes trouble.

You and Alex are adorable. I didn't know you were back together.

Hopefully this time ends better for y'all.

That last comment hits a nerve. Is there a reason to be petty on a post I'm tagged in. As for the others…it's times like this I wish I didn't live in a small town. They know way too much of our history. And why do they always jump to conclusions? Just because we're at an event together doesn't mean we're an item. Though, it does look like we're awful chummy.

The bell above the door rings, and I glance to see who walked in. Speak of the devil. Alex holds the door open for his daughter and another little girl. It's like I summoned him by thinking about him. Maybe if I keep my head down and act like I don't know them, they won't realize I'm here.

"Emily!" A small but excited voice captures my attention.

Well, there's no hiding from them now. "Hi, Kira."

"Did Daddy tell you we were coming here?" She glances over her shoulder at him and smiles.

At least, I know she doesn't dislike me. That could be a problem. "No." I laugh. "He didn't tell me you would be here. I came to get food for me and my friends."

"Us too!" She pulls the girl beside her closer to me. "This is my friend, Samantha."

"How cool is that? I have a friend with the same name."

"Really? That's so awesome." Kira catches sight of the room off to the side with a few games scattered through-out. "Can we go play while you order the food?"

"I already placed the order. We're only here to pick it up." His eyes meet mine. "But you can play for a little bit." He reaches into his pocket and gives them a few dollars.

"Thanks, Daddy." The two girls dash to the game room.

Alex sits in the chair next to me and nudges me with his shoulder. "Were you trying to hide from me?"

"Yes. No." I shake my head and groan. "Maybe."

"Why? Did something happen between the time I left your house this morning and now?"

"My friends interrogating me was fun. They're still at my house waiting on me to bring food."

"My parents tried to give me the same treatment, but Kira was in the room."

"Then social media is buzzing about us."

"What do you mean?"

I hand my phone to him. "Tiffany posted a picture of the Whoopsie Daisy crew, and there are so many comments."

"Most of these look like they are about the flowers." He scrolls further. "Oh. Well, I guess Mom was right."

"About what?"

"People finding out if we were together before we did." He chuckles and wraps an arm around me, pulling me close.

I let out a breath. "So, I'm not the only one who wasn't sure we were an item. I mean, I thought for sure after you said you weren't letting go of me again. But...I didn't want to assume."

He sets my phone down and reaches out for my hand. "We're really doing this?"

All the reasons we shouldn't float to the front of my mind, but right now I don't care. I want to give us a chance. "Yes."

His lips meet mine for a chaste kiss. We are in a public area after all.

"Are you boyfriend and girlfriend?" I jump away from him and almost tumble out of my chair. Kira is standing a few feet from us with a small stuff animal in her hands.

"Oh my God," I mutter and bury my face in my hands. This is embarrassing.

"Can you give us a minute, Samantha?" Alex asks Kira's friend. She nods and heads back to the game room. He motions for Kira to come closer. "Would it be okay if we are? We don't want to do anything to make you uncomfortable."

"Yes!" Kira claps her hands. "Grandma and Grandpa were talking about you yesterday. They really like you which means you are good people."

It's good to know his parents still love me, and now we have his daughter's approval. It's a relief and terrifying. Not because I don't know how to handle kids. I've been around Caroline's son since he was a baby. But I feel like I need to earn Kira's trust, and I'll do what I can to make sure it happens.

Alex shakes his head. I'm sure about his parents discussing me in front of Kira, but it's a hurdle we don't have to worry about. "I'm glad you approve."

"I have an order for Emily." One of the staff calls out from the counter.

"Kira, why don't you get Samantha. Emily's order is ready and I'm sure she needs to get back to her friends."

"Okay." She moves in front of me and gives me a hug. "This is for you." She sets the stuffed animal in my lap.

"Thank you so much. I'll keep him in my car with me."

She runs off without another word.

Alex gives me my phone and helps me from my chair.

"Well, you definitely have her stamp of approval. Do you need help carrying everything to your car?"

"No, you've got her hands full." I nod toward the girls walking toward us. "I can handle it."

He walks with me to the counter and kisses me on top of the head. "I'll call you later tonight once the girls go to bed." As I turn away, he calls out, "I want a copy of that picture. It's a good one."

He's not wrong. I just hope I can live up to both his and Kira's expectations. This is territory I've never been in, and I can't screw it up.

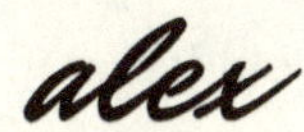

CHAPTER EIGHTEEN

"CAN I come to work with you today?" Kira asks me as I get ready.

"Why? You'll be bored and I don't want you to get hurt while I'm tearing things down."

She's sitting on my bed, watching cartoons. "So, I can see Emily again." It's been the topic of conversation for the last couple of days. While I'm glad she's on board with me dating Emily, I wish she wouldn't worry so much about it.

"You'll get to see her soon." Emily has to work a wedding on Saturday, but Friday night we're planning on taking Kira bowling. We wanted to surprise her, but my child is making that difficult.

"Promise?"

"Of course." I finish fastening my belt. "Why are worried about not seeing her?"

"Because she makes you happy. If she's not around you'll be sad again."

This kid sure knows how to punch me in the gut with

words alone. I think back over the past few years. There's not a moment where I recall being sad. Well, other than when I was looking at pictures from my past. At what could have been. Though, I'm grateful it's a possibility.

"How was I sad?"

She shrugs her shoulders and glances down at her hands. "You didn't smile as much as you do now."

"I'm sorry kiddo." I wrap her in a hug. "You are my reason for breathing. If I seemed sad, I wasn't. It was probably stress. But you don't have to worry. I'm happy as long as you are my daughter."

"Well, I'll always be your daughter." She rolls her eyes. "I guess I'll wait to see Emily."

"How about you and Grandma come up to the flower shop at lunch? If Emily isn't busy, we'll go eat together."

"Okay." She nods, knowing it's the only concession she's getting from me. I'm not sure how I lucked out with such an amazing kid, but I won't take it for granted.

"I have to go now. I'll see you later."

"Bye Daddy, love you."

"Love you, too."

I'll fill Mom in on the plans on my way out. Hopefully, Emily agrees to them because she's usually completely focused on the plans she writes down. Throwing something at her out of left field is likely to push aside whatever she has going on.

***

"How am I supposed to hold this again?" Emily struggles

keeping the sledgehammer upright. I don't blame her, it's heavy.

Moving behind her, I lift her arms and slip my foot between her legs to widen her stance. "It's pretty much like holding a baseball bat, but you have to even out the weight of the hammer."

"You know damn well I never played sports."

"And yet I see you at the ballfields all the time." I laugh and she leans into me. "I promise it's not that hard."

"I'm only there to support my nephew. I don't know what's going on half the time. The only thing I know deserves a cheer is when those kids make across the plate."

"You're hopeless." Shaking my head, I take a step back. "Now, all you have to do is swing. But try to hit where I drew an X. The last thing I need is you taking out a support."

"I think I'll feel better with you helping me."

"You only want my help so I'll be behind you, holding you." She grins and winks at me. I'm not that easy to fool. If we were here alone, it'd be different, but the building is full of people. There's no way they'd let us live it down if they came in here and we were making out, which isn't beyond the realm of possibility.

"Fine." She takes a step forward, adjusts the hammer and swings. Dropping it to the ground she moves closer to inspect the damage she's done. "It's barely a dent. That swing felt powerful enough to put a hole in the wall. What happened? I think your hammer is broken."

Picking up the sledgehammer, I inspect it. "Nope, I think it's an operator error."

"There's no way." She grabs the tool out of my hand and almost falls backward. "Let me try again."

This isn't going to end well. I take a few steps back and let her do her thing. Telling her no isn't an option. Once she sets her mind to something, she does it.

She gets back into the stance she was in moments ago and swings again. The hit isn't anywhere near the previous one. Now there are two dents in the wall. At this rate it's going to take a month to take the wall down. Frustrated she takes another swing. This time a tiny hole appears where the edge of the hammer met the wall. One more and another dent.

She blows out a breath and glares at the wall. "This is dumb."

"I don't see why Emily gets to take swings at the wall and the rest of us can't." Kate peeks through the plastic curtain I've put up to block off this area of the warehouse.

"Because I'm dating the contractor." Emily sticks her tongue out at her friend.

"Nobody said you can't." I roll my eyes. Sometimes being around all of them is like herding cats. "Whoever wants to help tear down the wall can do it."

Kate doesn't hesitate. She rushes toward the hammer and picks it up. She looks behind and holds her hand out to Emily. "I probably need those safety glasses."

Emily grunts as she hands them over and watches as Kate swings into the wall. The dent Emily put in the wall is now the beginnings of a hole.

"Yes." Kate throws an arm up in victory. "I demolished something."

"The only reason you got that bit of wall is because I already started it," Emily mutters under her breath.

I don't have the energy to get between them today. "Okay, I think I'll take over for now. Remember, the longer this takes the more the shop owes me."

"Would y'all leave the man alone and let him do his job?" Kai's voice booms from the hallway. He must have heard the part where I said it would cost more. "Besides, we had more orders come in. Two of them are rushes. It looks like Tiffany's post drove more business for every day arrangements."

"So much for things slowing down," Kate grumbles as she sets the sledgehammer on the floor. "Are you going to grab us some lunch since we have to work on rush orders?"

"Do I have a choice?" he asks now that he's at the edge of the hallway.

"Not really," his sister shoots back. "Besides, I'm older I get to tell you what to do."

"That's what you think. When we're at work you have no say over me."

"Ugh, siblings are annoying." Kate stomps off to the other room.

"I'm so happy I'm an only child." Emily laughs.

"Me, too." Before she walks away, I move in front of her. "Actually, Mom and Kira wanted to meet us for lunch today. I know you have orders that need to be made, but would you mind if they stop by and eat lunch with us? Kira is antsy to see you again."

"Why?"

"It's a long story."

"Oh, okay. I don't mind." She looks behind us at the hall opening to see if Kai is still there. "Who knows, maybe she'll think what we do is cool."

"I'm sure she'll have you trying to teach her how to make arrangements."

She taps her finger against her chin. "Actually, I'll see if we have any flowers, we won't use, for her to make one."

"She'll love that." I pull her in for a quick kiss. "I don't deserve you."

"Pfft. Just wait until you hear my request."

Now I'm terrified. But I'll do whatever she asks with no questions. Hopefully that doesn't come back to bite me in the ass.

"I think I want to be a florist when I grow up," Kira says from the table between Emily and Sam. Emily tried to put her on the other side of her so she wouldn't get in Sam's way, but she wasn't having it. She said she had to sit next to the person who shares the same name as her friend.

Mom decided to go grab lunch somewhere else because she thought she'd be in the way. Her brief reunion with Emily was like something you see in a movie. I didn't think she would ever stop hugging her. There may have been tears shed by both of them, but I won't mention that.

"I thought you wanted to be a professional softball player." I raise an eyebrow. Even though I know she'll never stick to any of these passions. Well, she might. The future is wide open for her.

"I can be both." She crosses her arms over her chest.

"Yes, you can." Emily bumps her with her shoulder. "Don't let anyone tell you otherwise."

"I didn't know you play softball." Caroline sits down next to me. "My son plays baseball, and he's only a few years older than you."

"Does he play at the same park?" Kira cocks her head to the side.

"Yep. Y'all may have games on the same night. If we do, we'll stop by and watch you play." Caroline smiles sweetly at her. Just like that, Kira is becoming a part of the group. If me and Emily have issues, we'll have to talk through them because no longer being a part of this will destroy Kira.

"Can we watch him play, too?" Her eyes meet mine, hoping I'll agree.

"Yep. Even if we don't have a game the same night, we can cheer him on."

"We even have our spot at the field," Emily says. "Everyone on our team knows we're the only ones who sit in that area."

"That's so cool. I want you to have your own section at my games."

"Oh, we'll make it happen." Emily moves a flower around the vase until she finds a spot she's happy with.

My phone buzzes in my pocket. "I think Grandma is

almost here, kiddo. Let's clean up your mess so they can get back to work."

"I'm not ready to leave yet." Kira looks at the small bouquet she's made.

Emily gathers a few supplies before standing. She crosses the room and empties a tote bag. When she comes back to the table, she holds the bag open and puts the supplies inside.

"You can take these home to practice. One day soon, we'll have a bouquet making party at my house."

"Deal." She sticks her hand out, waiting for Emily to shake on it. To Kira it's the equivalent of a pinky promise.

"I'll see you later, Kira."

"Bye, Emily." She wraps her arms around Emily's waist for a quick hug before she joins me on the other side of the table. "I can go now."

I love how she thinks she can dictate what she does and doesn't do. I walk her to the side door and Mom is waiting in her car. She must have text me when she was already here.

Once I have her buckled in her booster seat, I let Mom know I'll be home later. She assures me I don't have to come straight home. There isn't much for me to do, though. Emily has girl's night with her friends, and I know better than to infringe on that.

Everyone inside is back to work, and I head back to the sectioned off area to make progress on the demolition. I want to get this wall out before I leave. Then I can start framing up the new one. I still have to build an entire room from scratch on the other side of it. Luckily it doesn't have to be as big. It's times like this I wish I had a crew. It would make the process so much faster.

I'm not sure how long it's been, but it sounds like it's quieted down in the other part of the room. There are only a few bits of the wall close to the framing left for me to cut away. I glance at my watch and realize it's close to six. Wow, I guess time passes quickly when we're all busy. It also helps that I had music playing in my headphones. If anyone tried talking to me, I couldn't hear them.

Once the last bits of drywall hit the trashcan, I pull my headphones off and set them on the table. Walking toward the hall, I check to see if anyone is there. The lights are off in the front of the building and the office. Huh. Surely Emily wouldn't leave without saying bye.

I head through the plastic partition and see Emily putting finishing touches on an arrangement. "You're still here."

"Yeah, I needed to finish up a couple of orders before I meet the girls at the bar." She carries the vase to a refrigeration unit against the wall. "I wasn't sure you were ever going to be done."

"I lost track of time. But I have the wall out." I move toward the table and pick up the leaf clippings she's pushed aside. "So, what's the thing you need me to do?"

Her request has been bouncing around my mind since she mentioned it. The fact she didn't say it when everyone was in the shop means it's something I probably won't want to do.

"You're not going to like it." She comes back to the table to help clean it off.

"I already told you, I'd do anything you ask." I pull her close to me when she's close enough.

Her arms wrap around my neck and leans on her tiptoes to kiss me. It's demanding and if we weren't in the building I'd have in a bed in a heartbeat. But there's no telling if someone may come back to the shop for something.

She pulls away and her big brown eyes meet mine. "I want you to come to dinner at my parents soon. Maybe we can bring Kira as well."

She was right. I don't like it. But my hands are tied. I told her I'd do anything. This falls in line with that. Besides, if we're going to be together, her dad will have to like me at some point. We probably won't be taking my daughter with us until I know her dad doesn't blow up on me.

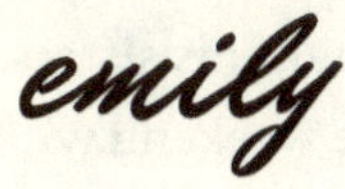

CHAPTER NINETEEN

THE ONLY PROBLEM with dating someone is our schedules are all over the place. It's so weird being with someone who not only has his work schedule but also a child's plans to think about. It shouldn't be weird because Caroline did it for years. She's also had a much harder time because of the hours Carlos had to work. He still goes in at night from time to time, but not as much as he used to.

My friends gather around me as I clean up my area. "Are y'all going to both games tonight?"

"Of course," Caroline says. "We told her we would. Now, you need to make us shirts to support her team as well."

"Why am I always the one who has to get crafty?" I cross my arms over my chest. "Last time I checked, we're all creative people."

"Because you have the patience," Samantha adds. "There's no way I could sit there and pull every little piece of vinyl off the sheets before ironing it on. That's way too tedious."

"All I hear is excuses." I wave them off. "We better go before we're late."

"Yep." Caroline nods. "Carlos is already there with David. I think he brought his sisters. David will be happy. He loves spending the weekend with his tias."

"You basically have them as babysitters while we work the weddings this weekend." Kate laughs. "I hope you're paying them."

"They won't accept it. I've tried. They heard Carlos talking about hiring a sitter while we both work on Saturday, and they offered."

"Why don't your brothers offer to watch him?"

"Reaf has his hands full with his kids, and I'm not going to make Bryce do it. He helped out a lot when he was growing up. Him and Delilah have a good thing going, and I don't want to interrupt that."

"You're way too nice to your siblings," Kate scoffs. "If it was me, I'd be forcing my kid onto Kai any chance I could."

"Which is why I'll never answer the phone when you have kids." Kai joins the rest of us. "I won't let you take advantage of me."

"No, but Vivian will." Kate smiles. "You know, if I were to have kids. But I like living vicariously through the rest of you."

Samantha doesn't add to the conversation. In fact, she's been awfully quiet. I'll have to dig into that later. Right now, we need to head out.

David's team lost by two points, but they fought hard. Caroline gave him the option to go home with Carlos, or stay and watch Kira play. He opted to stay with us. I swear that kid never gets enough of being at the ball-fields. I'm sure when he gets to high school he'll be there as much as possible working to get better.

Alex and his parents are sitting in the bleachers. I don't see how because they are beyond uncomfortable.

"We made it." I wave my free hand in the air. The other one is carrying my chair.

"I see that." He waves back. "Y'all come prepared."

Caroline sets her chair up next to the dugout, and Alex's eyes widen. She has one of those fancy collapsible rocking chairs. "When you spend every spare moment at a practice or game, you learn to appreciate the comfort of this over the bleachers."

"Oh, I like that." Alex's mom comments.

"I have an extra one if you want to sit in it for the game." She points to one of the chairs David is holding.

"Really?" She stands and scoots past her husband and son. "That's so kind of you."

David sets it up for her next to Caroline then whispers something to his mom. She relays the message, "David said he's going to sit on the bleachers with his friends if your husband wants to take his chair. Sorry, he's shy around new people."

"Thank you. I'm sure he'd love that." She waves him over and its only Alex sitting on the hot metal. The stands are under a small awning, but it doesn't do much to keep them cool.

"I feel kind of left out now." Alex grimaces.

"You can sit in my chair." I grin at him.

"Where will you sit?"

"In your lap."

"It's way too hot for that. In more ways than one." He winks at me and laughs. He's lucky he's handsome and I like him. Any other guy would have had a punch to the gut.

"Y'all are ridiculous." Kate rolls her eyes. "Xander, give Alex your chair."

"But..."

She doesn't give him a chance to respond. He does as she asks even though he groans about it. "Now, sit down."

As soon as he does, she sits on his lap. "How is this any different than what they were going to do?"

"People expect it from me." She shrugs. "And this is his daughter's team. He needs to be respectable around Kira, her teammates and the other parents."

Alex sits between me and them. "Wow. Did I just hear an adult response from you Kate? Things really have changed since I've been gone."

"Bite me," she retorts.

"That's more like it."

"Quit being mean to her." I slap his leg.

"Fine," he grumbles. "But the Kate I knew would have said all kinds of wild things when you said you were going to sit in my lap."

"When we were teens, maybe." I argue.

"No, he's right," Kate agrees. "Even five minutes ago. But I know how vicious some of these moms can be. Remember, we went to school with them and some of them are still judgmental assholes who don't mind their own business."

"She's not wrong." Alex adds. "Occasionally I get looks from people at practice. And that's nothing to say of some of the single moms trying to give me their number."

"Excuse me?" That ends now. I'm not normally a jealous person, but I just got Alex back in my life and there's no way in hell I'm losing to him anyone else. I scoot my chair closer to him and put my hand on his leg. Maybe this will stop them from trying to get with him.

His only response is to chuckle and put his hand on top of mine. He was probably trying to get a rise out of me, and it worked. Who cares if it makes me look like a possessive person?

"The game's about to start." He leans forward without moving our hands. He watches the girls run onto the field and take their positions. "There she is on second base." He points to the base in question.

"I know where second base is." I roll my eyes.

"Don't let her lie to you," Caroline calls over to us. "She waits to cheer until she sees us."

My friends suck. I wouldn't air all their secrets to their respective others. Not that it's a secret I'm not into sports. I never have been. Anytime we went to games in high school and college I was the one yelling, "yay sports." They would always give me grief over it because I was lost most of the time and they got tired of trying to explain it to me. Nothing much has changed.

"I can help you learn the game if you really want, but I won't push you," His voice is low to keep everyone else from listening in. It's the small things he does that makes me feel special. He knows when I can't handle getting picked on by my friends. Especially over something that doesn't really matter.

"I think I'm good. I'll let you know if I change my mind."

"Okay."

The game starts and the girls are hitting balls thrown by their coach. I vaguely remember it being the same with David when he was younger. The girl from the other team makes it to first base. I see Kira bend her knees by her base, ready for whatever action she needs to take. She was serious about being dedicated to the sport.

Her focus is on the batter, waiting to see which way she's going to hit the ball. It comes directly toward her and she grabs it off the ground and rushes to touch the base before the girl from first gets there. The umpire guy calls an out and I stand to cheer. I at least know that's a good thing.

Watching these girls play isn't as high energy as watching David, but that's because it looks like a lot of them are still learning. Maybe I'll learn a thing or two about the sport because it's at a slower pace for most of the game. I guess that's why the games are timed.

Kira steps up to bat and Alex pulls out his phone. I slip my hand from his so he can record. He hasn't done it for most of the game because he's been too invested in the outcome. She swings and a strike is called.

"It's okay, baby girl. Keep your eye on the ball. Only swing if it feels right."

I'm not sure how Alex knows all this. He didn't play baseball when we were in school. But I love that he's supportive of her without being a jerk. I've been watching some of the other parents and they are way too hard on their kids. They are young, let them have fun. Not everything has to be about what comes next. I suspect most of these parents are trying to live through their children and want them to get those successes they obviously didn't.

Their coach pitches the ball again. Kira swings and this time the bat and ball connect. It flies toward third base and hits the ground a few feet past it. She drops the bat and runs.

Alex's mom is jumping up and down. "Go Kira, you've got it. You're almost there." The other team throws the ball toward first base and it flies past it causing that girl to run after it. "Keep going Kira. Take it to second." She does as her grandma says and takes off. As soon as her foot hits the base she grins. "There you go. Good job, kiddo."

This is a side of his mom I've never seen before. Who knew she was such a sports fan? I didn't. Though the TV being on baseball games when we were younger makes more sense. I always thought it was because of his dad, but maybe that's the thing they like doing together.

I'm definitely interested in the outcome now. I pay

more attention than I ever have to anything related to sports.

Kira's team won by one point. I guess that's one of the perks of them being the last to bat. She huddles with her teammates as the coach talks to them and one of the parents hands out snacks.

My friends gather the chairs while me and Alex head to the group. I don't miss the way some of the moms' stare at mine and Alex's joined hands. I really wish some of the people in this town would mind their own business. We're back together. It's known we're the couple everyone thought would make it. We were voted that our senior year in the yearbook. It's been well over a decade since then. Some people love to keep their high school ways, I guess. We found our way back to each other and other people should be happy about that. Unless, of course, they had thoughts of dating him. Sorry, ladies, he's all mine.

The coach dismisses the girls and Kira runs toward us. "You came."

"We told you we would. The rest of the group won't always be here, but you can count me in when I can make it. You did great out there." I hold my hand up for a high five, and she slaps it with everything she has.

"I'm getting a home run before the seasons over." The determination she has is awe-inspiring. It reminded me of when I set my mind to owning my own business. Even if I was older when I came to the decision.

"I totally believe you will, and I hope I'm right here to see it."

"Is there anything you need to get before we head out?" Alex asks her.

"No?" She scrunches her face.

"Oh really? You don't need your bat or glove."

"I can't believe I almost forgot those." She runs toward the dugout to get her gear, but Alex's mom is walking out with both in hand. "Thank you, Grandma."

"Anytime sweetheart." She glances over at us. "Do you want us to take her home?"

"It's okay, I'll bring her home."

"Are you sure?" She nods in my direction. It's like she thinks I'm going to disappear. That would be difficult considering we live in the same town.

"Yes, Mom." Alex chuckles. "I'm hoping she'll tag along to get ice cream with me and Kira."

"As if you even have to ask. You know that's my favorite."

"You kids have fun." His mom waves and heads toward the parking lot with Kira's gear in hand.

"We're getting ice cream?" Kira screeches.

"Of course, you did great out there, kiddo."

"Awesome." She puts one hand in Alex's and the other in mine. "What kind of ice cream do you like?" Her hazel eyes meet mine.

"My absolute fav—"

Alex cuts me off. "Chocolate chip cookie dough. She eats all the dough bits before eating the ice cream."

"Dang, you couldn't even give me a chance to answer."

"Sorry." He winces.

"I don't think cookie dough should be in ice cream." Kira shakes her head. "The only good ice cream is chocolate covered in chocolate syrup."

"That's...a lot." I say in the kindest voice I can manage. My teeth hurt even thinking about that. She'll be in a sugar high when they get home. I feel bad for Alex when he tries putting her to bed. I have an inkling it'll take a while.

"With sprinkles," she adds.

"Maybe we go should go easy on the sprinkles tonight."

"But, why?"

"Because it's already late and you don't need that much."

"Fine." She pouts. "I guess chocolate syrup is enough."

I can't help the laugh that bubbles out of me. This kid is something else. She'll be really surprised when she finds out what we have planned for tomorrow night. I hope she's ready to beat her dad at bowling. From what I remember he sucked. Even though I'm not much better, I know I can beat him.

CHAPTER TWENTY

"YOU'RE HERE. Wait, what are you doing at my house?" Kira jumps up and down when she sees Emily at the front door.

I hope like hell nothing goes *south* between us because Kira will be devastated. She's gotten incredibly attached to Emily in such a short amount of time. I'm not sure if she's already looking at her as a mother figure because she doesn't have one and many of her friends do, or if she genuinely wants to spend as much time as she can with her. I mean, she has my mom...but there's quite an age difference there. Mom can't do all the things Kira wants to do.

"Well." Emily looks over at me. "Your dad and I have a surprise for you."

"I like surprises." She opens the door wider and motions for her to come inside.

We need to have a talk about her opening the door. Even though it's Emily this time, that may not always be the case. And, let's face it, my child is way too trusting.

"Me too," Emily says. It's a lie. She hates surprises. It takes everything in me not to bend over in laughter, and I almost choke trying to hold it in. The glare she shoots me could turn someone into ice. Not me, though. It may have been a while since I've seen it, but it still doesn't scare me.

I tried to surprise her for her birthday when we were in high school and she got so mad before she figured out what we were doing. So, I know for a fact she's not being honest. She'll also regret telling Kira she likes them because that kid is sneaky on a normal day. This statement basically gave her permission to try to surprise her.

Kira merely nods at the statement.

"Hey sweetie, can you get some shoes on so we can head out." She runs to the back of the house toward her room. "And make sure you have some socks!"

When I turn back around, Emily's eyes are traveling around the room. No doubt seeing if anything is different. She hasn't been here in over a decade.

"Not much has changed." She meets my eyes. "It still feels just as homey as it did when we were kids. The only thing missing are your parents."

"Mom decided they needed to have a date night."

"I love that even after all this time they still go out and enjoy each other's company." Sadness fills her eyes. "I don't think I've ever seen mine go out like that. At least, not if it didn't involve a work function."

The information doesn't shock me. I'm sure her parents love each other, but they never really gave off the super romantic vibes. Not like mine do. Which is why they've been so happy about me and Emily seeing each other. Mom said they are gaining their daughter back. Clearly, they thought we were going to be an item forever. Had I not been dumb way back then, we probably would have been.

Now we're starting over, but not from the beginning. We have to learn who we are as adults together. Though, she's barely changed. At least, from what I can tell.

"Mom hinted they'd be back before we get home from bowling."

"That seems like a very specific hint." Emily laughs and I want to hear it for the rest of my life.

"It was." I shake my head. "They want us to go out and enjoy time for ourselves afterward. She's adamant we don't need to take Kira to do everything we do."

"Will that be hard for you?" She moves toward me and wraps her arms around my waist. She looks up until her eyes meet mine. "It's been you and her on your own for so long."

She's not wrong. The thought of not being at work and also not being around my daughter is a hard pill to swallow. "It will probably be difficult. Don't be surprised if I turn into the type of person who shows off pictures of her and countless stories."

"That's fine with me." She squeezes her arms against me. "But we definitely need alone time. I don't think it's a healthy relationship if we don't. I know Kira will always be your number one priority, and I'm okay with that. Just make sure you make us a priority."

"You and Kira may be tied for number one," I mutter.

"That's good to know." She leans up toward me and gives me a quick kiss.

"Gross," a small voice says from the other side of the room. "Every time I walk in to a room, you are kissing or hugging."

Kira shakes her head in disgust and moves to the couch to put her shoes on.

"Sorry, kid, but you'll have to get used to it."

"Fine," she grumbles.

"But we can stop doing it as much. Would that be, okay?" Emily adds.

Kira sits prim and proper. "That would be great."

Shaking my head, I release Emily from my hold. "This kid will be the death of me."

"She's not so bad. Do you remember what we were like as kids?"

"When you put it that way, she's a saint."

Our group was always managed to find trouble without looking for it. Well, I take that back. Kate was always looking for trouble. Anything to piss off her parents.

"Are you ready to go?" I ask Kira.

"Yes. I can't wait to see where y'all are taking me."

"Let's just say, we're totally going to beat your dad."

Great, now Kira is going to be in competitive mode. If I don't do well at bowling, she'll never let me hear the end of it.

"Do I get a hint?" Kira asks as she makes her way toward us.

"Nope." I shake my head. "You'll see when we get there."

Once they are on the porch, I close and lock the door behind us. I hope Emily only plans on one game of bowling. But, if I somehow manage to win, I know Kira will demand a rematch to compare scores.

***

"Well...that was interesting." Emily is lying on her couch with a glass of wine while I'm making a batch of popcorn. We opted to hang out at her house after dropping Kira off with my parents. Both of us were ready to collapse. "How did she manage to beat both of us?"

Nobody ever believes me when I tell them how competitive she is. That may be the only trait she got from her mom. Everything was win or lose with her. I'm only hoping she grows out of it or she'll piss off a lot of her friends and teammates.

"When she sets her mind to something, she does it." I'd like to say it's a quality she got from me. But clearly, I've let other people influence me to make certain decisions. I hope to be more like Kira in that aspect. The things we can learn from children.

"To be young and full of excitement again," She toasts to the air and takes a sip.

"Are you saying we're old?" I call across the room. Her house having an open concept has its advantages.

"I don't think that word came out of my mouth," She yells back before grabbing the remote.

The kernel pops have slowed down and I stop the microwave. The cooking time is inconsistent on this thing. How in the world has she never burned her popcorn.

I dump the popcorn into a bowl, and head to the

living room. I have no idea what we're watching and I don't really care. Honestly, she'll be lucky if I manage to stay awake. Between working at the shop today and then getting beat by Kira, I just want to sleep.

Lifting her feet, I sit down. "You may not have said the actual word, but you implied it. Which is basically the same thing."

"Okay, let me rephrase." She takes another sip of her wine. "I miss getting that exciting adrenaline rush about something. Now, I'm just tired most of the time."

I feel her there. We both probably put in about the same amount of hours, except mine includes raising a child. But she's wrong about one thing.

"You're saying you don't get any adrenaline rushes at all? About anything?"

"Not really."

"Well, that's not acceptable."

I set the bowl of popcorn on the coffee table before reaching over and gently pull the glass of wine from her hand to join it. Sliding out from under her legs, I stand at the edge of the couch.

She's staring at me with wide eyes. Bending down, I lift her up in both of my arms. "What are you doing?"

"Giving you a rush."

"Oh." The word is a soft sigh as I carry her to her room. As much as I loved the spontaneity of the couch last time, tonight I plan on taking my time with her.

I set her down on the bed, and she stares at me, wondering what I'm going to do next. A part of me wants to make her wait with anticipation. But I don't know if I'm strong enough to do that.

Getting down on my knees I reach for the button on her jeans and pop it free before pulling the zipper down slowly. Her eyes are on me the entire time, mine on hers. If this doesn't give her those exciting feelings, she said she missed, I don't know what will.

My fingers curl through the belt loops and tug. She sets her hands down on either side of her and lifts her body so I can pull the jeans out from under her. When I have them down to her knees, she sits back down.

My focus is on her the entire time I take her pants off. She reaches out to me to pull me toward her, but I lean back. If she wants adrenaline...I'll give it to her.

Standing, I lean over her and guide her to lie down. She does without question. My lips meet hers for the briefest of seconds before a place a few along her jawline before working my way down. My fingers trailing along at the same time. I lift her hips to pull her pants down and throw them behind me.

My eyes meet hers as I settle between her thighs. She bites down on her lip and I know she's ready for me. My tongue brushes against her and her entire body shivers. Her legs squeeze me as my tongue works faster. Her hands fly to my hair and mine grip her thighs to keep her in place.

I'm lost in her. Basking in the reality that I get to have all to myself. She's mine and I'm hers, and I don't think anything could ever change that.

My name is soft chant coming from her mouth. Steady and full of longing. His fingers twist in my hair as she lets out a moan and comes apart. The taste of her on my tongue is the best way to end this night.

She wiggles out of my hold and grins. "You've proved your point. Now it's my turn."

I'm not sure what I did in my life to get another chance with this woman, but I'm grateful. Being in this bed with her every night is the only thing that could make my life better than it already is. I can't lose her... again.

CHAPTER TWENTY-ONE

THE PAST FEW weeks have been absolute bliss. Being able to see Alex every day is more than I can ask for. It helps that he's at the shop all the time working. With the help of his parents, we've been able to go on dates and spend quality time together. We also take Kira on as many adventures as we can within our schedules. This is what it's like to be an actual family. I've always thought what I had was the perfect family. Stuffy at times, but still it's the idea I've grown up with.

It doesn't compare to how I feel with Alex and Kira. There's a genuine love between all of us. As wild as that girl can be at times, she has completely stolen my heart. I'm a little sad she won't be going to dinner at my parents with us tonight. But it's probably for the best. At least for now.

I've pushed off dinner with my parents for as long as I could. They wouldn't take no for an option this week. It's taking me way longer than it should to get ready.

Uncertainty floods through me even though I know dinner with my parents and Alex needs to happen.

Am I ready to do this? I glance in the mirror one last time to check my outfit. Tonight, will either be a revelation with my parents or a disaster. I'm hoping for the former, but I probably shouldn't hold my breath.

We're supposed to meet at my parents in thirty minutes. I told him we could ride over there together, but he still had to go home and get showered. He said he also wanted to see Kira before the dinner. I love how dedicated he is to her. There's nothing sexier.

Wow. Did that thought just pop into my head? Never did I think looking at a father would turn me on. The only common factor is that it's Alex. I'm pretty sure I wouldn't have that thought about anyone else. Maybe it's because I knew him when we were young and seeing the man he has become has turned my world upside down.

My phone dings from my nightstand.

Alex: I'm heading out in about five minutes.

Emily: Sounds good. I should get there around the same time.

Alex: Kira says hi.

I snap a quick picture of me holding the stuff animal she gave me and send it to him.

Alex: She said he's supposed to be in your car to keep you safe.

Emily: Tell her he was helping me pick out an outfit.

Alex: Should I have her call you since you seem to want to talk to her more than me?

Emily: No. I'm sure I'll see her at her game.
Alex: See you in a few.
Emily: Bet I beat you there.

I know for a fact I'll beat him to my parents' house. He's worried about how my dad will react to us being a couple.

Taking him to the wedding as an act of rebellion is one thing. Dating him is another.

Alex is already waiting when I get there. He hasn't gotten out of his car yet. Hell, he isn't even parked on the curb right in front of my parents' house. He's across the street and one house over. Because that's not weird at all.

I pull into the driveway and before I have a chance to open the door, Alex is right there doing it for me. And they say chivalry is dead.

"Thank you," I say as I step out of the car. He closes the door behind me. "How did you get over here so fast? You're parked further away than me."

"What can I say, I was anxious to see you." He shrugs and slides his hand into mine. His palm is damp with sweat. It's hot out here, but not enough for this to be outcome of being outside for a few seconds.

"Are you nervous?" That would be absurd. My dad may not like him, but he's not a monster. He's perfectly capable of being civil.

"Maybe a little." From the stiffness in his stance and the grip he has on my fingers, I'm betting it's more than a little.

I turn to him before we head to the door. "Look, I know my dad can be...intimidating. But everything will be fine."

"You sure about that?"

"Why?"

"Your dad is glaring at me through the blinds." He glances down at me and tilts his head to the side. "They know I'm coming, right?"

This time I avert my eyes. Oh look, there's a flower growing through the crack in the concrete.

"Emily?" The worry in his voice forces me to make eye contact once again.

"Not exactly."

"Are you serious right now?" He lets go of my hand, takes a step back and runs his fingers through his hair. Frustration and anxiety warring with each other. "Your dad already hates me. This isn't going to help matters."

"They invited a guest to the last dinner without saying anything to me. Why can't I do the same?"

"Because it's their house. And, you didn't even stay when that guy was here." He throws his hands in the air and shifts part of his body toward the street. It's much easier to leave when you're already facing the right direction.

"That's the beauty of it, Alex. It's not like they can leave. They will be forced to hear us out."

I can see the itch to run written all over his face. Despite telling me he would come, now that he has new information he doesn't want to stick around.

Can I blame him? I wasn't exactly truthful when I

told him to come to dinner. But his reaction isn't something I expected, either.

He faces me once again. He's made his decision to stay and go through with dinner. "I'm willing to see this thing through, even if I have a bad feeling."

"Thank you." I wrap my arms around his waist and hug him. "You have no idea how much that means. If he acts like a jerk, just say the word and we're gone."

"Okay." He lets out a breath and squeezes me tight.

Sliding my hand in his, I give it a quick squeeze to let him know I'm here. Maybe we'll finally figure out what the animosity is between the two of them.

I lead the way to the front door and knock. It doesn't take long for Dad to answer since he was at the window moments ago.

"Hi, Dad. Where's Mom?"

She's usually right behind him when I get here.

"She's grabbing an extra table setting for your guest."

I don't miss the way he glares at Alex, especially when he sees our hands intertwined.

Alex slips his hand from mine and holds it out in front of my dad. "Hi, Mr. Hughes. It's been a while."

"Yes, it has."

He doesn't bother shaking Alex's hand, and after a few moments Alex drops it. Maybe he's right. We shouldn't have come here, but it's too late now.

I don't understand what went so wrong with these two. Not that Dad, has ever been Alex's biggest fan, but I don't think I've ever seen my dad be this disrespectful to anyone.

Finally, Dad takes a step back and lets us into the

house. This is the first time I've ever felt weird being here. Well, other than a couple of weeks ago when they tried to set me up with a complete stranger.

"Dinner smells delicious," Alex says to break the silence.

Mom walks in at the end of the sentence. "Thank you. Everything's ready and on the table." At least she's being pleasant. For some reason it feels like Dad is the only one with the problem.

We follow Mom to the dining room and take a seat. Instead of sitting in my normal spot across from my mom, I sit in front of Dad. It's probably best if I put a little distance between the two of them.

All of us stare at each other, unsure of what to do next. Why are my parents being so weird?

"Thank you for dinner, Mom." I reach across the table to serve myself since nobody else will.

"Don't be silly, I love cooking for you."

"It looks amazing, Mrs. Hughes."

"And tastes even better." She giggles. Dad glares at her for breaking ranks.

Alex serves himself and my parents do the same once we're done. We all begin eating even those it feels like all the walls are pressing in on us.

"So, Emily said you're doing the renovations at the shop." Mom saves the day with small talk.

"Yes, ma'am. I hope they like the final look." He glances at me with a small smile. Some of the tension gone from when we walked in. "Kira, my daughter, is excited to see it, too."

"I didn't know you had a child. How old is she?"

Mom's showing interest in Kira. That's good, at least. Maybe she'll stop bugging me about possible grand-children.

"She's six. So far, she's loving Asheville. She was able to get on one of the little league softball teams and we spend a lot of time practicing."

"I'm glad she's adjusting well. Moves can be hard on a kid." I know she's speaking from her own experience. My grandparents moved around a lot to follow the work.

"And your business? How is that going?" Now Dad wants to talk?

"It was going great before we moved here. I'm hoping I'll get more jobs after people see the renovation. Word of mouth is king in small towns."

Dad grunts, and I'm done with his rudeness.

"Is there a problem, Dad?"

"No, no problem at all. I'm just trying to figure out why he's back in your life when I explicitly told him to stay away from you."

"You what?" I shriek.

"With all due respect, Sir, Emily and I are adults. I don't think you can dictate what she does with her life anymore."

"How dare you?" Dad stands. I know that face. It's the same one he had when I was growing up and giving him attitude. Mom stares at the scene before her in horror.

Alex looks over at me, sadness filling his eyes. "I'm sorry, Emily. I can't do this right now. I don't have to take this from him, and you shouldn't either." He kisses the top of my head. "I'll talk to you later. Thank you for the meal, Mrs. Hughes."

I watch in horror as the man I want by my side walks out the front door. Tears welling up in my eyes because he's leaving once again, and I don't know what the hell just happened. I guess it's a good thing Kira didn't come tonight. This isn't something she needs to see.

"Y-you told him to stay away from me? Is that why he broke up with me in college?"

"That's not any of your concern."

"You know what?" I stand and lean over the table. "There was one thing Alex was right about. I don't have to take this from you anymore."

"Don't go, Emily." Mom reaches out to me.

"I'm sorry, Mom. I can't do this right now."

I make the same path as Alex and walk out of my parents' house. The hope I had that Alex would be out here waiting for me dies when I see his car is no longer parked across the street. I have no idea what just happened here, but I feel like my world has turned upside down.

Never did I think my dad would stoop so low as to micromanage my relationship. Or that Alex would freaking listen to him.

Getting in my car, I back out of the driveway. I don't want to go home. It's lonely there, and Alex may be waiting for me. I'm not sure I can handle talking to him right now. He's just as much at fault as my dad because he never said a word to me.

Before I know what I'm doing, I pull into Out of the Ashes. Is it the best decision? Absolutely not. But right now, I need to be alone in a group of people. I'll call my friends later because they are going to lose their shit. Especially after all of them have pushed us to get back together.

I couldn't even have this moment for a short time without one of the two people I thought would always support me destroying my view on the world. I can't help but wonder how else my father has steered my life.

CHAPTER TWENTY-TWO

EVERY BONE in my body is telling me to turn around. To go back and save Emily from being berated by her dad. But if I stayed there any longer, I would have ended up in jail. He has no right to talk to anyone like that. Walking out was the safest thing for all of us. I half expected her to run after me. To come to my defense after the way her father treated me, and how little he thought of her capabilities to make a decision, a decision as an adult.

But now she knows why I broke up with her all those years ago. It wasn't a choice I wanted to make. Back then I was young and easily intimidated. Her dad scared the hell out of me. I shouldn't have let him push me around, and I damn sure shouldn't have kept it a secret from her. But hindsight, and all that. Maybe she would have realized how manipulative he can be.

I couldn't though. Not then and not now. I'm not sure she would have ever believed me. She's always looked up to her parents. If I opened my mouth, she would have had to come to grips with an entirely new realization she never saw before. Emily needed to find out first-hand the asshole he can be. She had to witness it with her own eyes.

I hoped tonight would have ended differently. That we could put our past aside and be civilized. That he'd be happy is daughter is happy. But no, in the end, that's not what matters to him.

My knuckles are white from gripping the steering wheel so tightly. I'm kicking myself for not pulling Emily out of that house with me. I make the next turn and circle back around to do exactly that. When I come to the house, though, her car isn't there.

Now I feel even worse. She did come after me. I drive to the end of the road and make a decision. She would have gone home to come to terms with everything. I can apologize for...everything.

At least she had the good sense to buy a house on the other side of town. It doesn't take long to get there because it's Asheville. It doesn't take too long to get anywhere unless you live on the outskirts of town like I do.

Her car isn't here either. She could have gone anywhere. I would go to each of her friends' houses, but I don't know where they all live. Damn it. I let my anger get the best of me and now I can't apologize or comfort one of the most important people in my life.

She has to come home at some point, though. I'll wait for her. The neighbors have seen my car enough they won't think I'm suspicious. I turn off the car and sit on the front porch. It's still hot, but I don't care. My well-being is nothing compared to hers. When she gets back, I'll explain everything that happened our freshman year of college and how dumb I was back then.

⁂

Hours. That's how long I waited on her porch and she never showed up. I wouldn't have come home, but my mom kept calling me. When I finally answered she asked if she needed to pull together bail money. I assured her that wasn't necessary. My parents are the only people who knew what happened for all these years. I swore them to secrecy. Not once did they question my actions or stop loving Emily any less. They knew how much that information would hurt her and didn't want to inflict that pain.

Now, I'm standing at the front door, terrified to go in. Not because of how my parents will react when I tell them what happened. Though I'm sure they'll call me a dumbass for leaving without her, but I already know that. I don't need their confirmation. No, I'm scared Kira will be able to see straight through the happy facade I'm about to put on. If luck is on my side, she'll be fast asleep.

I slap a smile on my face and open the door. Fate is not my friend today. Kira is sitting on the couch watching a cartoon movie. I can totally fake my emotions and act like everything is perfectly fine. Never mind the fact I flunked out of theatre because I suck at acting. At least, I do when I'm face to face with someone. Back then over the phone...it was only possible because I couldn't see Emily. If I had done it in person, I wouldn't have been able to.

When the door closes behind me, Kira jumps off the couch. "Daddy, you're home. How was dinner? Is Emily with you?"

"No, sweetie. She had to go home so she can be up early for work. They have a busy weekend of weddings."

"Oh." her face falls. "Is she coming to my game Saturday morning?"

The fact I don't know how to answer that right now guts me. "I'm not sure kiddo."

She stops asking me a million questions and studies my face. "You're not boyfriend and girlfriend anymore, are you?"

"Why do you say that?" She's perceptive beyond her years. She may be rough around the edges at times, but she truly cares about the people around her.

"Because you're sad again." She runs up to me and gives me a hug. "And she made you happy."

"I'll give you to a minute," Mom says. I jump at the sound of her voice. I didn't even see her sitting in Dad's chair.

"Thanks." I give her a small smile. I know I'll have to let them know what happened. If anything, maybe they can give me some guidance.

I lift Kira up and carry her to the couch. To my surprise she allows it. She hasn't let me carry her in any aspect for years. She must know I need it more than she does. When I sit down, she cuddles into my side. "Does this mean I won't see Emily again? I really like her and her friends."

"No, sweetie. That's not what it means." Sighing, I run a hand through my hair. The amount of times I've done it tonight alone, I'll be surprised if I haven't actually pulled any hair out. "We had a disagreement. We're still together. Sometimes grownups don't act like grownups. Both of us need a little time to get our heads on straight so we can talk."

"So, it's like at my games when I get frustrated and start messing up."

"What?"

"You always tell me to take a deep breath, shake it off, clear my head, and try again."

How in the world did she get to be so wise? Though she's the only person I know that could equate my jumbled explanation to her softball games. At least she seems to understand the situation. This kid truly will take on the world and try to make it a better place. Even if she relates everything to softball. I couldn't ask for a better kid.

"It's exactly like that."

"Good. That means I'll see her soon."

I really wish I had the same level of optimism she has. Life would be so much easier.

"Why don't you head to bed? I'm about to climb into mine since I have to be up early in the morning."

She puts her hand on top of mine and pats it. "Do you want me to read you a bedtime story?"

Parenthood isn't supposed to work like this. It's my job to console her when her heart is hurting, not the other way around.

"It's okay, kiddo. But if I need you to tomorrow night, I'll let you know."

"Okay," she slides off the couch. "I love you, Daddy. Everything will be okay."

All I can do is nod. Right now, I don't know if it will. The world feels like it's crushing down on me, and nothing I do will make the situation better. I let Emily believe it was something she did that pushed me away. When it's all because I couldn't stand up to her dad back then.

I'm about to get up and head to my own bed, but Mom walks into the living room and sits down in the recliner. She doesn't say a word, just waits until I'm ready to tell her what went down. I'll be lucky if she doesn't march down to their house as soon as I'm done and demand an apology. God help him if she runs into him while out and about. It won't be pretty.

Whoopsie Daisy is the last place I want to be this morning. Confrontation isn't something I'm great at...obviously. Especially since I'm at the shop she co-owns, surrounded by her closest friends.

Technically I don't even need to be here. The job is pretty much finished. I only have to put a few final touches on one of the areas. Then I can take pictures and be out of their hair.

Hopefully I'm here early enough that nobody has showed up. Emily typically pulls into the lot about thirty minutes before the shop opens at eight. I'm here an hour and a half before that. Kira was still asleep when I left.

No cars are in the lot when I pull in. I should be able to get in and out of here without running into anyone. I unlock the door and let myself in. The alarm starts beeping, and I punch in the code Kai gave me.

My tool belt is in the new meeting room, and it's the first place I head. I fasten it around my waist and begin my inspection. There's a spot in the corner that needs a pain touch up, and I make a note of it on my phone. I check the light switch to make sure it works properly.

Every detail of this room and the one next door needs to be looked at. There's no way I'm going to give them a reason to be dissatisfied with anything in case things go south with me and Emily. I wasn't lying when I said word of mouth is powerful in small towns. This shop and the women who run it are beloved by this town. All it will take is one negative comment, personal or professional. I remember vividly how smalltown living works. Most people will believe what they heard from their hair stylists' neighbor's daughter before they'll come to the source.

Shoving those thoughts away, I focus on the task at hand. Right now, I need to keep every hope alive that we can work through whatever happened yesterday. I know she has to be pissed at me for various reasons. I'll feel better when I can talk to her. But this place isn't the setting it needs to happen. Getting lost in my work is what needs to be done to keep my thoughts at bay.

"You're here early." Caroline startles me and I drop the paintbrush in my hand. "Oh my gosh, I'm so sorry."

"No, it's fine. I didn't hear you come in."

"The renovation turned out amazing." She studies the new office area. "The minute you're done, I'm going to start decorating."

"You already have stuff picked out?"

"Yeah." she laughs. "We've been holding a lot of it in the garage at our house."

"I didn't even realize. Do you need me to move it in?"

"No, you're good. You got this done in record time. I thought it would take months."

"It moved along a lot faster when Emily and Kate stopped fighting over who was going to take down the wall." I try to look around her to see if anyone is lurking behind her. "Is, uh, Emily here yet?"

"No, she's not coming in today."

"But you have a wedding to prep for."

"It's fine. The rest of us have it handled. She said she's not feeling great."

"Oh." All the hope I was using to carry me through the morning deflates. "Should I go check on her?"

"I would give her the day." She comes closer to me and rests a hand on my shoulder. "Everything will be okay. She just needs to wrap her head around a few things."

"That makes sense." I guess. I can't blame her. When I hauled ass out of her parents' house it was basically for the same reasons. "I'll check on her in the morning after Kira's game."

"Does everyone know about my epic fuck up last night?"

"Only me. I had to pick her up and take her home.

Please know she doesn't place the majority of the blame on you. It's just a lot."

The first part of her sentence sticks in my head. "You had to pick her up? From where?"

Indecision flashes across her face. She doesn't want to tell me. "The bar. Carlos called me and said she had a couple of drinks and looked upset."

"Thank you for making sure she got home safely. I waited on the porch for a few hours but figured she was with y'all when she didn't come home."

"No worries. That's what family is for." She gives me a hug. "You're family, too. Talk to her tomorrow when she's feeling better."

"Okay." My heart is in vice. All I want to do is run to her and take care of her. But I'll respect her wishes. It's the least I owe her.

CHAPTER TWENTY-THREE

WHAT IN THE hell is that pounding sound? I sit up, ready to answer the door when I realize it's my head. I don't even think I drank that much last night. I was drowning my sorrows and spilling my guts to Eric, the head bartender. He's really good at listening. It must have been because I went straight for the liquor instead of my normal beer or wine.

I bet Alex is worried sick. I had a few missed calls from him, but I couldn't bear answering the calls. Not in the state I was in last night. When Caroline dropped me off last night, she told me not to worry about prepping for the wedding tomorrow. Hell, she even told me not to worry about the setting up the wedding.

She's right though. I have a lot to figure out. Not so much when it comes to Alex. I need to apologize to him for not coming after him. I wish I would have and I hope he can forgive me, though he has every right not to. Thinking back, I should have known something was off when he left that message in college. It was out of character for him. My gut must have known otherwise I would have already been in another serious relationship.

I glance at the clock by my bed. Almost one? I've never slept in this late. I need to find him so we can talk. As soon as my feet hit the floor, I know moving so quickly wasn't a smart idea. My talk with him will have to wait. At least for a bit longer.

Lying back down, I close my eyes. This headache needs to go away. I have bridges to mend, and I can't do that when a jackhammer is going full force on my brain.

My bed dips and my eyes fly open. I must have fallen asleep again. The person sitting beside me isn't who I expect.

"Mom, what are you doing here? How did you get in?" I purposefully didn't give my parents a key to my house out of fear they'd let themselves in whenever they felt like it. Like now.

"I came to see how you're doing." She takes a breath and lets it out. "I stopped by your shop and got a key from Kate."

"I'm fine." I wonder if she ran into Alex while she was there. He had to finish a few things before he could mark the job done.

"I can see that. How's the hangover?"

I side-eye her. "There's no way you can know I had a hangover."

"You're in bed at five thirty. There's only one other reason besides heartbreak for that."

Her being here isn't helping anything. "Look if you're here to apologize for Dad, I don't want to hear it."

She motions for me to scoot over. My people pleasing

ways keep me from rebelling. I move over and she climbs all the way onto the bed with me. She wraps an arm around my shoulders and pulls me to her. She hasn't done this since I was a kid. I wish I knew what changed in the years between then and now that she stopped being affectionate, even though I have an idea.

"I'm not here to apologize for your father. Well, not entirely. I'm sorry I let you endure that type of behavior for so long. I didn't know anything about the conversation he had with Alex."

"If you didn't like the way he was micromanaging me, why didn't you stand up for me? Why didn't you put a stop to it?"

"Because mija, I thought one day you'd defy him. But...you never did." It's nice to hear the endearment from her. It's been so long since I've heard it. But that doesn't negate the fact that not taking up for me was wrong.

"That shouldn't have been on me to do. My entire life the only thing I've ever done is try to prove that I'm a good enough daughter for y'all. To make sure you were proud of me." I didn't realize that's how I truly felt until the words tumbled from my lips.

"You're right, I shouldn't have left that for you to do." She lifts my chin up so I can see her. Her eyes are shiny with unshed tears. "Don't for a second think I'm not proud of you. You are the greatest gift the universe has given me."

"Why have you stayed with Dad so long? Neither one of you look happy." The sadness in her eyes has only gotten worse over the last couple of years, and maybe I should have been more observant. But I'm not the parent...she is.

"I've been planning on filing for a divorce. But I wanted to make sure I had enough money put away to get a place of my own." I didn't realize she was doing that. "For the longest time I didn't think I should leave. Your grandparents would get into fights sometimes and then work through it. For them, marriage is forever and they probably shouldn't have stayed together either. I thought if I worked hard enough, things would get better."

"But they never did?"

"Not exactly. We never really argued until you were in high school. He never liked Alex. When I confronted him about it, last night, he said he saw Alex as a threat to your future. He could see how much you loved him and knew you'd throw away everything you worked toward if it came to a choice between your future and Alex."

"That wasn't his call to make. I was grown and in college. Starting Whoopsie Daisy has always been my dream and Alex supported that. He wouldn't have done anything to put it in jeopardy."

I'm fuming. The audacity of my dad to think I'm not capable of making my own decisions. I've always been the most level-headed one in my friend group. When problems arise, I'm the one who fixes them. The fact he had so little faith in me hurts.

"I know that. I told him the same thing." She hugs me to her tighter. "I know I haven't been the best mom, or most supportive, but I do want what's best for you."

"I know, Mom. I love you, too." I squeeze her back.

"What are you going to do now? He can't be happy that you called him on his bulls— crap." No matter how mad I am at the situation, I still can't bring myself to curse in front of her.

"I went to a lawyer this morning to start drafting divorce papers before I went to the shop looking for you."

"What?" It takes me a few minutes to register what she's saying. "Mom, if it's not something you truly want to do, don't do it on my behalf."

"Emily, last night was the last straw. Especially after the argument we got into after you left. I've never felt so helpless, and I should have jumped in to fight for you."

"Did you happen to see Alex when you were at the shop?" It's selfish of me to ask, but I need to know. She nods. "Was he mad?"

"No. He was mostly worried. I also apologized to him for not knowing what was going on."

"I'm sure he understands. His beef is with Dad, not you."

"I was complicit, and that's enough."

"I need to go talk to him." I move to get up, but she pulls me back to her.

"No, you need to rest and recover. Your emotions have been all over the place in less than a day." When I try to protest, she shakes her head. "Tonight, I'll stay in the guest room and make your favorite for dinner. We can watch sappy movies and reconnect."

It may sound silly, but this is the closest I think I've ever felt to my mom and I hope it's something we can build on. "Um you'll have to go to the store to get the ingredients. I don't have the stuff on hand because you never taught me."

"I guess you'll learn tonight." She kisses me on my forehead. "Take a shower. I'll be back in a bit."

I watch my mom leave my room, admiring her for the bravest thing I think she's ever done.

This plan is ridiculous, but I think he'll appreciate the gesture. A stack of poster boards and a bluetooth speaker sit in the passenger seat of my car. It's also super early and I don't even know if he'll be awake, but I have to do something to show how much I love him. If he doesn't accept my apology that's on me and I'll deserve it. But he came back into my life for a reason, and I want to spend the rest of mine with him and Kira.

I pull into the driveway of his parents' house and put my car in park. Deep breath in and out. I'm glad he doesn't have any neighbors because this could be embarrassing if he rejects me. Turning the car off, I grab my phone from the cup holder.

Emily: Come to the door, please.

I don't wait for him to answer. I open my car door and pull my supplies from the seat. Setting the stuff on the roof of the car, I shut the door as quietly as possible.

A few moments later, I have my phone connected to the speaker and "All My Life" is softly drifting from it. I don't want to wake up his parents either. If he doesn't come to the door, it'd be nice to bask in my unsuccessful glory without an audience.

The sun is already beating on my skin, and good God would he hurry up and come to the door. Or text me and tell me to kick rocks. I shuffle through my signs to make sure they are in order. The last thing I want is the message to be messed up.

Finally, the door cracks open and I can see him standing behind the screen door. His hair is disheveled and I know he rolled out of bed. He moves to open the screen door and I shake my head. He tilts his head to the side and looks down at the large white paper I'm holding. It's now or never.

I look down to make sure he has time to read them.

I'm Sorry. I throw the sign on the ground.

I'm an asshole. Another toss

I should have. To the ground it goes.

Ran after you.

Please be patient

With me

I love you

And want to

Spend my forever

With you.

Before I have a chance to put the last sign on the ground, he's in front of me lifting me into his arms. His lips crash into mine and he spins me in a circle. I think I have my answer.

"You have nothing to apologize for, and you're not an asshole. I should have told you what happened. But he said if I didn't end things, he'd pull your college funding. I couldn't let that happen."

"Okay, he's the asshole." I never want to leave Alex's arms. "So much so my mom is divorcing him."

"Are you serious?"

"Yeah, she came to check on me and we talked for a long time. She stayed the night last night."

"Wow. I don't even know what to say."

"Me either, but she seems lighter than she has in years. It's like the weight has fallen off her shoulders."

"I know that feeling." He sets me back on the ground and looks around. "Did you literally recreate our freshman year of high school with all the romance movies you made me watch?" He takes a moment to listen to the song I have playing on repeat. "We used to skate to that song."

"I know. I'm pretty sure it's our song."

He kisses me one more time. "You have no idea how much I love you."

"Emily! You're back!" Kira rushes out the door and off the porch crashing into us. "We can all be happy now."

Her words send a pang to my chest. It wasn't just Alex's heart on the line. It was hers too. "Yep. I'm back. Sorry I wasn't feeling well yesterday."

"Are you coming to my game this morning?"

"Yep." I bend down until I'm the same height as her. "You have me all day." I glance up at Alex. "I was thinking after your game, we could grab lunch and go back to my house. There's someone I want you to meet."

"I love meeting new people. Who is it?"

"My mom."

"Awesome."

"Yes, it is. She makes excellent food."

I shake my head at him. That man is always thinking with his stomach, not that I blame him. Her food is amazing.

"I need to get ready for my game." Kira waves and heads back inside. "I know we're going to win today. I can feel it."

"Do you want to come inside? Mom and Dad will be happy you're here."

"Absolutely." I kiss him one more time. I truly can't imagine my life without him in it. He is and always has been the rock in my life aside from my friends.

He helps me pick up the signs and I throw them in the backseat. "I hope you aren't getting rid of those. We'll need them as proof to show our grandkids one day about how you tried to win my heart back."

"What do you mean tried? I'm pretty sure, I do have you back."

He shakes his head and bops me on the nose. "You can't get back what has always been yours."

epilogue

"WHERE'S THE BIRTHDAY GIRL?" Mom calls as she comes through the door.

"I'm here." Kira rushes toward her with a hug.

"Can you show me where to put your gift?" She knows exactly where they go. She helped us set up last night while Kira was with Alex's parents. Kira nods and leads her to the back door. I swear that girl has everyone wrapped around her finger.

It's great seeing my mom happy and enjoying her life. She bought a house a few streets over. Neither of us has anything to do with my dad. He hasn't attempted apologizing to either of us. As far as I'm concerned, he can live with the regret of not getting to know Alex and Kira. It's his loss.

I check the snack table to make sure everything is full. Once that's done, I head to the backyard where my friends and family are gathered. The only person not here is Alex. It shouldn't take him his long to pick up a bag of ice. The store is literally five minutes from the house. He's been gone like thirty.

I pull my phone out of my back pocket and dial his number. It rings and rings before going to voicemail. Worry settles in the pit of my stomach. There's only one other time he hasn't answered the phone, and even though we've worked past that drama, I can't help but wonder if something happened. That's the only possible reason he could have for not answering my call. What if he was in an accident?

"Mom," Kira calls over to me. It's still odd for me to hear it. She called me Emily for the longest time and woke up one morning calling me Mom. But I'm grateful she sees me as a mother figure, I would do anything for her. "Can we open presents?"

"Let's wait on your dad. I know he won't want to miss it."

"I'm here." His voice comes from behind me. He has two bags of ice in his hand and carries them over to the ice chests.

"What took you so long?"

"The gas station was out of ice," he grunts as he breaks up the ice. "I had to go across town to get it."

"Oh."

Before I have a chance to turn around Caroline is bringing out the cake. The candles aflame and sparklers sticking out of the top. I start singing Happy Birthday and everyone joins in. Caroline sets the cake on the table and when we're done singing, Kira takes a big breath and blows the out the candles. Alex pulls the sparklers out and snuffs them out in the dirt.

"Okay, you can start opening them now."

Kira doesn't hesitate. She rips wrapping paper off boxes and throws tissue out of bags. At least she takes the time to read any cards that are attached and thanks the gifter.

There's one late gift. It has the wrapping paper I used on her other gifts but I know I didn't wrap that one. As she starts pulling the paper off, music flows from the box.

No. No way. She pulls a speaker from the box and comes to stand by my side. I turn to look at Alex and he's down on one knee. "All My Life" playing from Kira's hands.

"I could make some longwinded speech, but we all know that's not me." A few laughs erupt from our friends. "Emily, I've loved you since we were fourteen. I can't imagine a universe where you aren't a part of my life. Will you marry me?"

"I don't know, that seemed pretty longwinded to me." All I get is an eye roll from him while everyone in the yard is trying their best to hold in their laughter. I guess I can put him out his misery. "Yes, goofball, I'll marry you. But it's pretty sneaky of you to use my own tactic on me."

He stands and slides a diamond ring on my finger. "What can I say? I learn from the best."

Within seconds he has me in his arms, and dips me backward. His lips meet mine and even though I've always felt fulfilled with my life...it's now complete. We've come full circle and there was a bit of heartache, but I wouldn't trade it for anything. Not when him and Kira are a part of my life.

"Best birthday ever!" Kira throws her arm in the air. "But can y'all stop kissing now?"

Alex lifts me up and gives her a high five. "Thanks for the assist kiddo."

She smiles and takes off to play with the other kids. Our friends and family clap and cheer. I couldn't ask for a better life.

acknowledgments

Wee One better be happy I love her. I almost dedicated this book to sleep so maybe I'd get some now that it's done. Seriously, sleep...I miss you.

Steph & Ashley, thanks for always being my cheerleaders when I need to get the words in. I seriously don't know how I would get through this without the two of you. Mel & Leigh, I'm so happy we're friends. I can't wait to work on awesome things with you!

Hubs, thank you for taking over the cooking while I was handcuffed to my laptop. It meant a lot! Boy Child, thank you for not talking to me when y'all knew I was writing. And giving me a laugh when I needed it. And Baby E, you are the cutest distraction when I need a break, and even when I don't. Being your gamaw is the biggest honor.

Readers, bloggers, and anyone else who picks up my books. Thank you! You have no idea how much you reading my words means to me. You are the reason I keep doing this day after day. Oh, and the voices that won't leave me alone. Seriously, thank you for joining my characters on their journey.

Do you want to meet more of the characters in Asheville? You can check out my books here. Or, scan the QR code to find out what some of the other residents of this small town are up to.